20/40

by

Stephen Leininger

20/40

by
Stephen Leininger

20/40

Printed by CreateSpace. An Amazon.com Company

This is a work of fiction. Any reference to actual persons, entities, or events is coincidental or is used fictitiously and is not intended as a statement of fact.

Printed in the United States of America.

http://www.stephenleininger.com

ISBN-13: 978-1495349799
ISBN-10:1495349799

This book is dedicated to you, the reader. It wouldn't exist without you. Actually, it wouldn't exist without me. Way to go, me.

But seriously, thank you.

PART ONE

CHAPTER ONE

This is the third funeral I've attended this week, and it's only Thursday. No, I don't know three people who have died this week. Throughout the course of my life, in all its twists and turns, there has been something lacking. So I trudge my way through the lives of the dead, gathering information. Enticing events, becoming enthused. The opportunity to see how someone else lived out their life, and how I could never hope to live out anything as spectacular. But I can imagine how amazing and wonderful their life must have been, and I can, for one small moment, put myself in their shoes—within my imaginary paradise of having a beautiful, meaningful life.

There is also a second, much smaller adventure, of lying. This only happens if a family member decides to approach me and inquires after my relationship with the deceased, and I am given an opportunity to spin a tale of a strange misadventure we shared together eons before, leading the relative to learn a lie they never knew about their beloved.

The large throng of people around me are all dressed in black, standing in groups, afraid to be alone. And then there's me, standing alone, afraid to be in a group.

This funeral is held outside. It's broad daylight with a handful of clouds in the sky, barely creating any relief from the sun. The tent over the grave provides the pastor and family members with shade.

Jamie, the deceased, died a few days ago, only twenty-four years old. Jamie's morning was standard: waking up at eight-thirty, hitting the button on the coffee maker, returning to her room to set out her clothes for the day, then heading into the bathroom to turn on the water for her shower, turned too quickly, lost her footing and smacked her temple into the corner of the vanity.

She lost consciousness, and remained there for an hour.

She was found by a worried assistant who went to her home to check on her. Jamie survived for three days.

Jamie was a girl who spent every weekend traveling. She had met so many people through her office over the years that there was always someone in a different city to visit. She'd leave every Friday night, only packing an overnight bag and arrive back on Sunday evening just in time to get some sleep before the work week began again. She was an up-and-coming agent at a talent agency. Celebrities filled her address book. From the pictures, she was beautiful. She had a knack for being in the right place at the right time. Except that morning.

It amazes me how such a full life can be extinguished so quickly. And makes me wonder how I'm going to go out. Easily? Maybe. But then, we never were meant to understand everything in life.

The mother bursts into tears, the father puts an arm around her.

I stand there awkwardly, trying to look sad. My mind wanders throughout the whole service, even as the father stands in front of everyone to share with us something about his daughter's life.

"..Someone as bright, and as charming as my daughter," he sobs.

She really does sound like a sweet girl. Ghosts of tears are clinging to my eyes while the people around me are openly weeping for their far more personal loss. There seems to have a larger turnout when someone dies young.

Jamie's father regains his composure. He'd only said a few lines, but I didn't expect him to make much of a speech. I'm surprised anyone says anything. Personally, I have never spoken at a funeral, even at the ones I was *supposed* to be attending.

My mind wanders back to this morning. After breakfast I dressed and walked out the door. I knew where the funeral was, but not much else. From driving up the thin paved surface in the graveyard, to deciding where to stand, to talking to the right people. It's nerve-wracking, and only certain people can do it.

I hear a car door shut and I turn to look. A young woman with dark hair, around twenty-five years old, approaches the tent and stops a few feet in front of me.

We've been standing in silence for over a minute now. At least 50 pairs of tear-glazed eyes follow the casket as it's lowered into the ground. The casket arrives at its final destination at the bottom of the grave, and the people gathered start drifting away.

Before I turn to leave, the woman in front of me starts to shake from crying, and I'm hit by a wave of empathy. That's odd. I've never felt so much for someone else in pain. I start walking, trying to remember where I parked my car. The dark-haired woman quickly passes by me, and in her haste, still sobbing, trips and falls over a rock. I rush forward, take hold of her arm, and help her back to her feet. She briefly glances at my face, mutters a "thank you," and the three of them rush off again.

I spot my vehicle, and somberly walk towards it. I sit in my car for a minute, thinking about Jamie's life; Going to work everyday, getting a paycheck, interacting with people every two minutes, making a difference. In contrast, here I sit, in my car, daydreaming about someone else's life.

I follow the long line of Cadillacs and BMWs in my own modest Ford around the quiet cemetery until we're back in sight of bustling society, and I break off from the group. I glance at my watch. I imagine Jamie walking down a sidewalk in the middle of the day, being recognized by everyone that passes. I'm on the other side of the street.

No one notices me. They're too distracted by the beautiful girl.

Cars pass me, going the other way. I look out the window and see a park, barren and gray. It'd be perfect in Spring. I make a mental note to come back then.

**

Dad looks at me sideways, smiling, and looks back at the ground in front of him.

"Don't tell Mom that you're here, please?" I ask,

"Of course not," he says, chuckling. "She does mean well."

"She can do better," I say.

"Oh come on, that's not fair," he says. "Your entire life away from home, who's tried to keep you grounded? Who called you eight times a week and tried to keep you close as much as possible?"

"Mom, but-"

"Exactly," Dad says. "Your Mom."

"But she never tried like you try," I say.

"Love is a weird thing, and–"

"And Mom has a weird way of showing it," I finish. "She's definitely not Mom of the Year."

"And I'm not Dad of the Year!" he says. "Just like your Mother, I'm far from perfect kiddo."

"You never once thought of me as a failure."

"Neither does she," he says.

"But she acts like she thinks I'm a failure."

"The definition of success varies from person to person. I taught you that *years* ago. Us old people are like that," he says.

"Mom has never been happy with me."

"As a child? No." We stop in the middle of the walkway, trees towering over us on either side. He looks straight into my face. "I was never able convince her that you were equal in status to your brother. But now she's *trying*. Actually trying. And you're standing here feeling bitter because you're stuck in the past."

A disgusted chuckle sputters from my mouth.

"Now you listen to me," he says, poking two fingers into my shoulder. "Because this is the truth. You spent years being mistreated by your Mom and I tried to pick up what she didn't. Sometimes I still think I didn't do a good enough job raising you and your brother. Your Mother sees her mistakes and she's trying to catch up on what she missed as a parent. Those phone calls and invitations are her apology, and you have to accept that. You know your Mom. You've gotta meet her halfway, because that's all she's got. Don't you think she deserves a second chance?"

We stand there in silence, his challenge echoing in my head.

"She had her second chance, and a lot more on top of that," I say.

"At least try, will you?" he says. He's staring into my eyes.

"For you, I will."

He claps me on my shoulder. "Good. Now let's see about that lunch you promised me."

CHAPTER TWO

My apartment is on the fourth floor of a twenty story building. When you walk in you're greeted by my living room, with rooms that branch out on either side of it. The room on the right is my kitchen, which is partially walled off, creating a counter so that there can be a bar with stools on the Living Room side of the wall. The room on the left is my bedroom.

Less than five people, including my parents, have seen my apartment. I prefer it that way. I live alone. I'm not pining for company, though. I'm perfectly happy living alone. I don't want an uninteresting roommate, and I don't want to be saddled with a girlfriend. As Groucho said, "I wouldn't have anyone who'd have me!"

I close the door and turn the four locks, and place my wallet, keys, and phone on the counter.

As I start to eat my lunch, I wonder how the dark-haired woman was feeling. Putting aside her obvious sadness, bursting into tears in public, and then falling down can't have been good additions to her day. It's nearly one o'clock now. I clean up after lunch and walk into my living room and sit down in the middle of my sofa.

I have several pieces of furniture in this room, not a lot, for a small apartment. I have a sofa, two comfortable chairs, and my TV sits on a coffee table. I also have a dining table, surrounded by four chairs, behind the sofa. I rarely watch TV.

I admit, I myself am something of a pathetic being, but a being nonetheless. Just because I lack the ambition to seek out a wonderful, fulfilling life like the many I've seen buried doesn't mean I'm not human. Admittedly, it's not a normal human quality to go to funerals.

Life: One. Derek: Zero.

My name is Derek. I'm twenty-five years old, six feet, two inches tall, dark brown hair combed to one side, brown eyes, two eyebrows, ever so slightly bearded, high school graduate. I'm currently employed at a local bank as a part-time processor. I'm an ex-playwright. My days are indistinguishable from each other except for my visits to the funeral parlor.

I have no friends to call me, so I'm surprised when my phone rings. The caller ID says Mom. I let out a sigh of exasperation and pick up.

"Hey M–"

"Derek, sweetheart," Mom cuts me off. This happens often. "Your father told me you didn't have anything to do tonight, so I thought I'd let you know that your brother is coming by for dinner, and he's bringing Kelly and the kids!"

Mom's voice, telling me that my brother is in town, is not what I want to hear. I'm not a big fan of my family. Now you know. A sigh of exasperation runs through my head.

"Hello to you too, Mom. Good to hear from you. How did Dad know I wasn't doing anything?"

"You two had lunch yesterday, sweetie!"

Oh, yeah. I worked yesterday morning and ran into my Father while shopping for groceries (or as my Dad says, "Fridge-Fillings"), so we briefly met for lunch. It's possible that I told him I was free tonight. I can hear my Mother breathing over the line. Seven years out of school and she still can't entertain the possibility that I have no interest in most other people.

"Oh, that's right. I forgot. So," I begin, "as for tonight, I suppose I could come. What time should I...?"

"We're eating at six, but show up anytime you feel like, honey!"

I can barely contain my excitement.

"Okay, Mom. I'll see you tonight. Tell Dad I said, hi."

"I guess I'll let you go then. See you tonight! Love you!"

"Love you too, Mom," I say. "See you then."

I toss my phone aside and it clatters on the floor. I don't own a smartphone. It's a one piece, half a keyboard, makes phone calls, and, with some effort, can text. My computer isn't even that new, at five years old. Probably needs an update, but I don't use it much anyway. It just sits there.

I need to kill four and a half hours. I get up, don my jacket, pick my phone up off the floor, grab my keys, wallet, and walk out the door. I know what you're thinking: No, I am unable to lock all four locks from the outside. One of them is a chain and you only try that once, and after you spend a quarter of an hour awkwardly holding your arm inside your apartment, while the rest of you is on the other side of the door, you realize that it's a futile business, and you decide it's time to just sit down, and eat pie.

The weather has warmed up since I was out this morning. I step forward from the building and I run into a woman. I sit up on the concrete and look around. People have stopped to stare at me, and some are helping the woman get back to her feet. She's dressed completely in black. I stand up, almost tripping over my feet, and losing balance and falling over a second time. I ask her if she's okay.

I see her face—it's the dark-haired woman from the funeral! She looks up at me.

Neither of us say anything for a few moments. We just look at each other. All I can think is how uncomfortable this is. What am I supposed to do? Part of me now wants to yell "I'm sorry!" and run back inside, lock all four locks on my door, and not come outside for a month.

I'm such a social butterfly.

"I'm fine," she says.

Before I can do anything, she turns and runs in the other direction. And then she's gone.

Now I'm standing in a crowd, far from alone and definitely not where I want to be. I do my best to be suave, and walk away from the scene. Five blocks later, I stop and walk back home, realizing that the crowd is probably gone.

I lock all four locks, and change into some more comfortable clothes. My watch says three thirty-four. Can't I just sleep or something? Wait, why not? This is brilliant! I set my alarm for two hours, lay face down on my bed, and fall asleep.

My eyes snap open as soon as my alarm clock screams its distinct buzzer that I know and despise so well. My watch now says five twenty-five. I need to go. I brush my teeth and make sure my clothes aren't so wrinkled that my mother would immediately notice.

I don't want to be early, or even on time, so I keep driving around for an extra few minutes to give me time to think. After five minutes, I've thought about nothing. I pull up to the house. One minute past six.

My parents live out in the suburbs in a fairly new development. My feet carry my body to the house and my hand raises itself, knocking on the door a few times. We usually just walk right in. Now I feel stupid. Battling my indecisiveness, I walk in.

The front door opens right up to the TV room, which consists of a large flat screen TV (due to my father's love of baseball), and at least two couches so that any other company that decides to drop by, day or night, will have a place to sit. Behind the TV room, is a bathroom, and directly left of the TV room is the dining room, where my family is waiting.

I hate this place. Both of my parents, my brother,

and his wife, are sitting at the table, food already on the table and steaming, clearly waiting for me. My mother stands up and hugs me, and she asks if I had slept in my clothes the night before.

I try not to roll my eyes, and force a smile. My brother stands up, welcomes me and hugs me. I reluctantly hug him back.

"Hey, Derek," he says.

"Hi, Marshall," I reply.

Marshall is three years older than I. He's Mom's favorite. Graduated high school early, then graduated college early, and then started his own business. Now he's rich, and lives in the house we grew up in. Oh, and he got married and had two boys. Marshall married his dream girl, Kelly.

I nod to Kelly who smiles and says hello. That's fine, I didn't expect much from her. My Father gets up, shakes my hand, and tells me I should sit down with them. I'm only here for him. He's genuine.

The food's getting cold, he says, his gruff tone coming out a little stronger than usual. Must be getting nervous. I don't blame him. It's been a while since we were all at the same table. Especially for dinner.

Marshall's boys are Tim, who is five, and Jeremy, who is four. They're very rambunctious, as one would expect boys to be. The two boys run into the room, kick me in the legs, and run back out. It's unclear how they feel about me.

Mom has always been very traditional about family gatherings. She sets the table just right and fixes a large meal, whether it was for one relative or twenty. I put a little bit of everything on my plate, and start to eat. My parents tentatively follow suit, and my brother and sister-in-law share a nervous look, then do the same.

Silence.

No one wants to be the first to speak. I'm content

with filling my stomach with the delicious food on my plate. My brother clears his throat and asks me how work is.

"It's fine," I say, "my boss continuously demonstrates that he needs to be either demoted, or fired. Preferably fired."

I actually like my boss.

"That sounds very entertaining. I was up in my office this morning…"

My brother's office is a room in his house. *What a snob.*

"…and I found one of your plays from high school, Derek."

I look up. I haven't written anything in a decade. There was a girl I liked at the time, so I wrote a romantic comedy. I didn't let anyone read it, for obvious reasons. It was the last one I wrote before quitting.

"Which one was it?" I ask, praying that it's not the one I'm thinking of.

"*Factory Street,*" he answers.

Oh no.

"Is that a fact?" I reply, trying to sound like I'm not seething, livid that my brother, my pretentious, duplicitous, supposedly hard-working brother found the one play that I was happy with. Is this the part where I'm supposed to be pleased?

"Yep," he says.

Kelly lets her mouth show the bare minimum, a shadow of a smile.

"It was great," he continues, "I finished it last night."

He touched my stuff. He. Touched. My. Stuff.

I'd like to clarify: I do love my family. I find them annoying and overbearing most of the time, but I love them. I hate my brother. He's the worst thing to ever happen to me. He's a bully, and he enjoys it. I'm trying not to be angry. He's trying to sound genuine, but I've known him forever.

"When do I get to see it on Broadway? I'll want to call up Jenny Williams and let her know you're famous," Marshall voices what I'm sure is what he considers to be his greatest blow, hoping to send me over the edge.

Maybe he wants me to freak out on the outside too. Maybe he wants me to pick up my fork and stab something. Maybe he wants me to yell. Maybe he wants me to abandon sanity and have me admitted to a mental institution. He's going to get what he asked for.

"Oh really? Maybe," I start, eager to tear him apart, but I turn to Kelly instead. "How long is Marshall's money going to keep you around?"

My Mother gasps, my Father laughs and silences himself after a glare from my Mother, Marshall garbles an unintelligible response, Kelly says something along the lines of "how dare you." I'm tired of this. Now I feel like screaming. I stand up, thank my parents for having me, and I walk to the door, where I stop and look back at them.

"Really. Thanks for having me. It's been fun."

And I leave.

I drive for a few blocks, turn right, then turn left again, and I pull over. I put the car into park, and I yell. I keep yelling. I yell until my lungs hurt. I inhale, and I yell some more. I scream out Marshall's name. As I yell, I slam my hands into my steering wheel, honking by accident. I sit up after a moment. I put my hands on my face, and when I remove them again, they're wet. I wipe my eyes, clear my throat which is now sore, put the car into drive and I leave.

I drove faster than I should have. I close the door, lock all four locks, and jump into bed, ready for sleep.

It's only seven thirty.

CHAPTER THREE

My eyes open as I wake up late the following morning. I must have slept through my alarm. I didn't dream. I continue to stare up at the ceiling, but it's backwards. I'm laying in my bed upside down. My neck is sore, but my feet, having been resting on my oh-so-luscious pillow, are very comfortable. I sit up, and look around. My phone is on the floor. I don't remember placing it there. I pick it up, and turn it on. Seven text messages, and five calls. They're all from Mom. The messages are all alike, only varying between "Where are you?" and "What happened?"

The events of the night before rush back to me.

Marshall read Factory Street.

This time I'm able to keep down the anger, and push it away. I have better things to do. I do my best to clear my head as I get ready for my day.

While I shower I remember last night, trying to do so with honesty. No bias, no anger, just thinking about it all, as it really happened. I truly believe that Marshall was doing his best to goad me and make me lose my temper, which I did. Marshall won.

My Mother actually wants me to be a normal person and make an effort with my brother, despite how he treats me.

My Father has always been good to me, but now it's hard to tell what he's doing.

The calendar on the kitchen wall says I have work tonight. Great.

After breakfast at twelve I leave the apartment. Marshall will be home. Home, for Marshall, is an hour and a half from my apartment. I don't touch the radio at all. Just silence.

I close the door to my car and I walk up the newly sculpted path that leads, winding, to the front door of the Marshall and Kelly Wilson residence, almost unrecognizable as my childhood home. I knock twice. The door swings open seconds later, and Marshall is standing there.

"Before you say anything, I'm sorry for how I acted last night. I shouldn't have said anything about your job, or your wife. It was way out of line." I pray my apology works.

"This could have been a phone call," my brother answers.

"I also came because I wanted to pick up my work and take it home."

Marshall smiles. He beckons me in. It doesn't look like Kelly is home. I'll have to apologize to her another time. Marshall leads me all the way up to the fourth floor, and then to the attic. I look around, and see many things from my childhood. From toys, to projects, to failed experiments, to furniture. Marshall says that it's right there. I look, and there it is. A short cardboard box sits in the middle of the space, filled to the brim with paper. Paper that's been written on. All my beautiful work. I pick up the box, and we head back downstairs. I thank him, and leave.

I know I'm far from okay with my brother, but it's a start, I tell myself.

It's a long drive back to my apartment, but I got what I wanted, so I can live with it. I turn on the radio this time. I don't even care what plays. I'm too excited to care. I'm eager to reread the pages that I wrote years ago. Reading your own writing is like visiting an old friend. You remember your adventures, the love you once had, how close you used to be, and you wish you could be that way again.

And sometimes you should let the past stay in the past.

When I'm close to home, I grab a few plays out of the box and walk into a coffee shop to read in a comfortable environment outside my living room. Before I find a booth, however, a woman walks straight into me. She had just walked in the door, and there we both were. It's the dark-haired girl from yesterday. At least she didn't fall down this time.

She smiles when she sees me, excuses herself, and walks in the other direction. I shrug, grinning, and find a booth. I arrange the plays on the table across from me. I look out the window, gazing across the street at my apartment building. I look back, about to reach over and get one of my scripts to read, but there's a figure standing over me.

"Oh, hi." She's nervous.

The girl that continues to run into me is standing next to the table.

"I'm Samantha, but you can call me Sam. Nice to meet you." She tentatively stretches her hand towards me, and I shake it.

I say nothing. She sits down.

"I feel bad about running into you so much," Samantha says. "I'd like to get you some coffee or something to make up for the trouble."

She wants to buy me coffee. I'm unsure how to feel about this.

"Uh, sure."

Samantha stands up, a smile forming on her face, and for a moment I forget all else, stunned at how beautiful her smile is. She reminds me of someone I could only have written about.

She walks back to me a few moments later, and sets a cup down in front of me. As she sits down, her arm sweeps the table, knocking the plays onto the floor.

"Oh I'm sorry!" she says, scrambling to pick them

up.

She picks up *Factory Street*.

Great.

I anxiously reach out for it, and as I stand I knock over my coffee. Thankfully, the lid was tight and untouched. By the time I recover and I look back up at Samantha, she's finished reading the first page. She's still smiling.

"Is this yours?" she asks.

She's looking at me, and her smile disappears.

"I shouldn't have read that. I'm sorry." She puts the script back on the table and slides it across to me.

I remain silent, examining her face. She looks genuinely intrigued by what she read. I decide to give her a chance.

"Normally," I start, "I'd hate that someone was reading it. Finish the first two scenes, and then let me know what you think."

What am I doing, letting someone else read my work? Something must be wrong with my brain today. The thought doesn't stop me from pushing the script towards her.

Samantha slowly picks the script up and opens it.

She continues to read, and I wait. The expressions on her face change often. I'm prone to throwing many emotional twists into the pages, so I'm not totally surprised. After two or three minutes, she looks up and sighs. It's a sigh of contentment.

"Wow," Samantha starts, "That was really inter-esting. I liked it a lot."

I smile.

"Do I get to read the rest?" she asks.

"Depends. How long can you wait?" I reply.

"Wait for what?" she asks.

"For me to type up another copy."

"As long as it takes," she says.

"Good. I'll try to have it as soon as possible."

She smiles, and hands the script back to me, but not before scribbling her number in the corner.

But I don't type up *Factory Street*. I start writing something new. I write for four hours straight, take a break, and then write more. I write until my fingers hurt from all the typing; I haven't used a keyboard in so long. My fingers nearly give out, but I'm finished, and now it's five AM. I collapse into bed.

CHAPTER FOUR

I didn't go to work last night. Didn't call in. Just came home and turned on my computer for the first time in nearly three months. Typed for hours on end, with breaks for snacks and trips to the bathroom. I only slept five and a half hours last night. I still don't know what I was doing. I'm not sure I want to know what was going on. I feel like I need to know, but I can't.

Samantha. She's expecting a newly typed copy of my best script. Of course, my best work had been done when I was still being picked on for having a squeaky voice, so how great could it really be? I need to read it again. Refresh my memory.

But here, I have something new. Not only that, but something finished. I had written an entirely new script in one night, and it's done. I'm impressed with myself. Who am I, that I can do that now? I get up from my chair: my body and my mind gently poking me, wondering when I'll know what I'm doing.

Maybe tonight.

Right now I have other things to do. I have to read *Factory Street*. I pick up the lone copy, walk to the comfiest chair in my living room, sit down and my eyes linger on the cover page for a moment before opening it and reading.

I remembered my first line of dialogue, even after the near decade since I last laid eyes on the phrase:

She always was one for trouble,
and she had the scars to prove it.

Barely a script.

Poor formatting and poor dialogue aside, I loved it. It was so full of teenage angst, and truth, and love, that it almost couldn't be from my brain. And yet here it is, in all its glory, before my eyes. Re-reading it, it is still as wonderful as I remember. It astounds me that I had written anything like it.

Now, two hours have passed. Still sitting in my comfortable chair in my Living Room, I had finished reading. From the first line of my character Julia being a scarred individual, to the last line of Julia breathing the lone word "Yes," answering the inevitable question of whether or not she would become the wife of Dalton. Dalton, the man who lived alone on *Factory Street*. Dalton, who wasn't looking for love but then ran into Julia by very nearly running her over in his car and wound up taking her to lunch. Yes, the astonishing amount of cheese in my script was intentional.

I toss my script onto the sofa and stand up. As much as I loved it, this script is now obsolete; I had written something new. I had started and finished a script last night. What I wrote hours ago was ten times better than *Factory Street*.

I grab my jacket, keys, phone and wallet, and I leave.

I lock all the locks.

Just yesterday afternoon I was across the street in the cafe, where I had encountered the peculiar girl Samantha, who was the catalyst of the hammering of keys by moonlight. Samantha's face crept into my mind. She really was a beautiful girl, odd though she was.

I notice that my phone has rung twice since I've been walking, and I remember I missed work last night, so I know my boss will not be happy. I take my phone out of my pocket, and I'm correct. The caller ID displays my boss' name. I pick up.

"I can't help but notice that you weren't here last night," he says.

"I noticed it too," I say. "I have decided to pursue something far more fulfilling than standing in a bank. I'll see you at the office, never."

And I hang up.

I just quit my job. My lone source of income. I've got to be dreaming. Or at least, hallucinating. I'd rather be dreaming. I'd rather have a job. I'd rather be sitting alone in my apartment reading. Or writing. I've stopped walking. I'm not sure what's going on in my brain. There's no way I can think straight right now; I'm far too tired. I rub my eyes, and go home.

I waste no time in emptying my pockets onto the bar, and heading straight to my bedroom where I take off my outer clothes and jump into bed. I don't care that it's still daylight. All I know is that I need sleep.

And then, there was peace. The solace from writing has finally found me. Pure, unadulterated peace. That's not to say that everything is suddenly perfect, because it's not. Far from it, actually. I'm sure this is a very short respite, but so far it's nice to have.

CHAPTER FIVE

I waste an entire day poring over my old scripts, and hating them. I have an idea. I open the window and fling my scripts through it. I watch as they sail down to the backyard of the apartment building, landing in and around the fire pit, and I close the window.

I go to my office and on the laptop and printer. I open up a word processor. This is something small. I only type for a minute or so. Some editing here and there, and some different effects with the fonts and general design. I print out just one copy. It looks decent. Well, as good as I'm going to get. I'm good at writing, not making invitations. I print out thirty more, and close my laptop.

I quickly leave my apartment without locking it, and dart around my apartment building, sliding one invitation under every door. The invitations are to a Winter bonfire in the backyard, by a complete stranger.

Fifteen minutes later, I'm back at my door, with several papers still in hand. I set the spare pages on my counter, and leave again to buy supplies. I quickly check my watch. I'm running late.

The grocery store is only a seven and a half minute drive away from my apartment building. I'm there in six. I go straight to the meat aisle. Ribs. Steak. Hot dogs. Handburger? That's not right. I definitely read that wrong. *Hamburger*.

In ten minutes I have everything I need, including skewers, straight from the clearance rack. I pay and head back to my apartment building. The invitation said Eight-thirty PM. I'm cutting it close.

The fire pit is located in the center of the courtyard behind the building. Not many places in the city have fire pits. This might be the only one. There's also a picnic table close by the fire, and stacks of chairs against one of the walls, next to a stack of pallets and firewood, underneath a tent to keep them dry. I put all the supplies on the table next to the fire pit.

Starting the fire is easy, even if I did it wrong. I crumple up a few pieces of paper, and stack the thick manuscripts around them. I light four or five matches at once, and stick them into the midst of the crumpled pieces of paper. Within moments they're turning black, and the edges of the full manuscripts are starting to light. I need more material. I can't just burn up these pages. I grab two pallets and balance one of them on top of my pyramid of paper.

The pyramid is burning pleasantly. My watch reads eight twenty-seven. Three minutes. Not that anyone would show up at precisely eight-thirty. There are few people who feel like showing up on time to any event, let alone an extraordinarily short notice bonfire. I stoke the fire for fifteen minutes before I get hungry and open the pack of hot dogs and rolls. When it's done I carry it to a picnic table a few yards from the fire. I can stay warm, and still enjoy seating. I'm on my third hot dog before anyone shows up. It's a man and a woman, holding hands. They brought lawn chairs with them. We say our hellos, and they set up their temporary seating a few feet from the fire. It looks like they're having their date night by firelight. Not a bad idea.

Five hot dogs now. What? I'm hungry. Another person walks into the courtyard. Guess who. That's right. Sam. I turn and focus my concentration on my seventh hot dog and try to look busy.

"Derek Wilson."

I turn around. Sam is standing two feet away from me. I have to give her points for recognizing me in such dim lighting.

"Nice jacket," she says.

"Please, sit down."

She does.

I ask her how she knew about the bonfire. She says that a flier was shoved under her door. Now that I think about it, I don't know any of the tenants, so for all I know, this woman lives next door. I excuse myself for a moment while I put another pallet on the fire.

"How long have you been living here?" I ask, sitting down next to her so that we're both facing the fire.

"A year and a half," she answers. "You?"

"Five years. It's been quite the adventure."

She tilts her head. "Oh yeah?"

"You have no idea how difficult it is. Cleaning all the furniture two times a day. Buying your own groceries. Refraining from turning on the TV. It's all just so hard."

Sam smiles.

"I can certainly see how that'd get annoying very quickly. Especially after five years. Very repetitive." She continues my joke. I smile too.

Sam looks at me, with a curious look on her face.

"So, disregarding the fact that you haven't given me a copy of your script yet, I'm wondering something, that is, if you don't mind."

"First, I have to know what it is you're wondering about, for me to mind anything," I respond.

"How did you come to live here?" she asks. "It's not exactly the nicest place."

"Ah," I say. "My family was overbearing, so when I was eighteen I moved out. I was broke and lived on a friend's couch for a while. When I got a job, I wound up here and never left. I live an excellent distance away from my brother, and a perfectly adequate distance from my parents. How about you?"

She says. "Well, for starters, mine also had to do

with a relationship. I had a boyfriend back home."

"Which was where?" I ask.

"Boston."

"Long way from here."

"Yeah. We were together for five years, and by the end, I just needed to escape. Everyone else seemed to know he wasn't a very nice guy but it took me a long time to figure that out. Even after I realized what he was, I still didn't leave him for nearly two months. I was just... like that. Wasn't sure if I'd have that chance again. Eventually I knew what I needed to do. I left Boston, then lived in New York for a year to do something different, and then I came here."

She stares into the fire as she talks. A tear runs down her face.

"Are you okay?" I ask.

She looks at me. Another tear falls to the ground.

"It still stings."

She looks back into the fire.

"I left everything; everyone. Hoping for something different. New York was such a failure. And in the short time I've been here, I've been to five funerals. That's more than I ever went to back home. I had been thinking that maybe there was some place better, and I just hadn't found it yet."

"Got anywhere in mind?"

"Maybe Florida," Sam says.

"Sharks can be nice."

"Yes, lovely creatures."

We both smile again. She looks at her watch.

"On that note, I should probably head to bed. I have a long day ahead of me tomorrow," she says.

"I'm going to sit here for a bit more."

"Sounds like a plan." Sam stands up, and stretches.

She takes a few steps, turns around and looks at me.

"Don't be a stranger. I'll try not to be so overbearing. Just so you know: five-oh-six."

She's gone. And now I know where she lives. Which is not a creepy thing to say. At least, not in this context.

I'm not going to lie, I had fun. I enjoyed my hot dogs and I had a short, but good talk with the girl who had seemed to be stalking me. I look around. The fire is dying, the couple is gone. I didn't even notice. I'm sitting by myself, around a pile of embers. My work is destroyed, and I'm alone. Right now, all I can do is sleep.

CHAPTER SIX

I'm dreaming. I'm *dreaming.*

I leave my apartment, and step outside, not even bothering to put on shoes. The air outside is crisp and cool. Not cold enough for my jacket, which falls from my shoulders onto the ground. Snow's falling. I don't know how long I've been walking. I wind up standing outside Marshall's house. Marshall himself is standing on his porch, higher than I am, his head down. As if he has no argument to make. No disconcerting thought against me. A woman comes up from behind him, and stands next to him. She looks unfamiliar to me, but Marshall holds her hand, looks into her eyes, and kisses her. And she kisses him back.

As they continue to kiss, someone comes up and holds my hand. It's Samantha. She smiles, and starts to walk, leading me away from Marshall's awkward embrace with the stranger. I don't know how long we've been walking, or even how far. Eventually we stand in the middle of a street in front of a run-down house. This street feels vaguely familiar, but I can't place it. There aren't any landmarks, just this lone house, two stories, broken and boarded up windows. The door is supported by a single hinge on the lower half of the door, so that the door itself hangs awkwardly to the side.

Samantha releases my hand and walks ahead so that she stands in front of the house. I follow, standing just behind her. She turns, and wraps her arms around me. I stare up at the house. I put my arms around Samantha, and she looks up at me. I squeeze her tighter, pulling her in closer to me, until our faces are barely an inch away from each other, and–

I open my eyes. My ceiling has never looked so

boring before.

I'd seen Samantha last night—Wait. Samantha. My stomach twitches.

I feel like I've been attacked by some monstrosity, like a parasite infecting my body, my emotions. At this moment, I realize that I haven't been to any funerals this week. But why? I shake my head, trying to clear the thoughts that aren't supposed to be there.

I seem to be getting closer to the realization I have feelings for this girl. But this isn't some fairy tale. This isn't a movie. People don't fall in love overnight.

I haven't even had breakfast yet and I'm trying to figure out the first real crisis I've had in years. I need some sustenance before I could even consider anything so important and potentially life-changing, but hopefully worthless.

I had the weirdest night. Not even the dream itself, but the fact that I was dreaming at all. I mean, I know that everyone dreams, but I never remember my dreams. Not in the last seventeen years, and the first one I get, stars my brother locking lips with a woman who just happens to not be his wife, and me who almost kissing practically a stranger.

I'm a little unnerved, which is reason for at least a small amount of worrying. That empty feeling in my stomach is still there, despite breakfast. I can't figure out what, but something isn't right.

And then it hits me: I haven't been to any funerals in a week.

I go to my front door, glancing through the peephole to make sure the coast is clear. With one swift movement, I swing it open, grab the tightly rolled paper, and close it again. I scan the obituaries for any funeral dates. Only one funeral is listed today. It's not too far away, though I have barely an hour to get there.

Looks like today will be rushed.

I jump in the shower, get dressed. I put on my dress coat, and walk out the door.

The motorcade is pulling away from the church as I arrive. I creep up behind the car in the rear of the line, and put on my flashers. During the game of Follow the Leader I try to remember what the obituary had said.

Jared Cummings, 38, husband to Sherri, and father to Lilly and Maci, was killed outside his home on Factory Street by a hit and run driver. The funeral will be held at 47 Bakers Drive at 11:30 AM, and the burial will–

I skip the rest of the obituary and concentrate on my driving.

The procession starts to slow down as we come to the cemetery. As I drive through the gated entrance, I see the employees setting up, preparing to add another body to their silent collection. When I finally park I'm almost at the bottom of the hill. I lose count of the cars lining the path. I work my way through the crowd, muttering Excuse Me's when necessary, but remaining silent for the most part. I don't want to stand too close to the grave, but I don't want to stand too far away.

A group of men and women follow the pallbearers walk by me. I assume these are Cummings' family members. I count four men, and six women. Only one woman in the group doesn't have tears in her eyes, but you could tell she had been crying. The group stops on the other side of the grave. Everyone, except me, is here because they lost someone they love, or they're here to support others who have lost someone they love.

Sam.

Nope. Not here to think about her. I have other things on my mind. This would be a terrible time for my phone to go off, right as the Priest is standing up to say his final words. Absolutely awful. I slide my gloved hand into my pocket, and attempt to silence my phone.

"...gathered today to say goodbye to Jared, and rejoice in the blessing that this man of God is finally happy, and finally home, spending the rest of eternity with his Heavenly Father."

Beep.

I hit a button. I tapped something. I'm not sure what, and I'm don't think anyone heard it, but I hit a button. My fingers search for the Home key, so I can try again.

Found it. A moment of fumbling, trying to press down the button, and I succeed. My phone is officially silenced. I return my attention to the funeral. The Priest finished speaking about Jared, and no family members say any final words. I understand that. A graveyard attendant steps forward and nudges the lever with his foot, lowering the casket into the ground, my eyes following it's movement.

Six feet under. So rests Jared Cummings.

A minute passes, and I'm still staring at the grave. Even the family members, close friends, and their emotional support have started the trek back to their cars, to congregate at someone's house, to fill up their living room to talk about Jared and what they used to do together, and all the memories they've shared, or they might even just go home to sleep, or drink, begging to escape reality for a few hours.

And even now, standing next to the coffin, supposedly saying my goodbyes to dear Jared, I can't get the idea of kissing Sam out of my head. This isn't what I want to be visualizing while standing over a dead guy in a grave. Actually, now that I think of it, I'm not sure what anyone should be visualizing when standing over a coffin.

I walk away.

This was a waste of time. I'm too distracted, too tired, too stressed, with too much thinking, and I was late. I never got to the viewing so I still know nothing about Mr.

Cummings. I'll have to research and find out the proper details for my next go.

By the time I arrive back at my apartment my mind is less clogged. I walk into my office and take the lid off of a large packing box. Inside is a stack of magazines, concealing a large stack of obituaries from the newspaper. I place Jared Cummings' on top, place the magazines over them to hide them and I close the box again. Right now, all that's on my mind is that I need another shower. I'm cold, so I start running water before I even take off my coat.

Christmas. Christmas is next week. I really don't have a special connection with Christmas. I don't visit any family—or friends, for that matter. That's not to say that I'm not invited to anything. My Mother always attempted to coax me into showing up at her house, but then I'd not only have to be face-to-face with my gloating brother, but the rest of my obnoxious family who think I'm a failed-writer-turned-alcoholic with financial problems as well. Of course, now that I've quit my job, the financial instability might be accurate in the near future. For the record, my Father was always accepting of whatever I decided to do come Christmas morning. Don't get me wrong, I don't ignore my family. I send them a card every year. My parents send me one back, with a fifty dollar check. The only other Christmas card I receive is from my bank, though I doubt that will happen this year.

CHAPTER SEVEN

My week wound up passing very quickly. With no distractions from work, and not having heard anything from Sam (or even seeing her), I was able to get a lot of writing done. I've been ordering food in, I haven't gone out, I haven't gone to any funerals, I haven't done anything. So I should go out.

Five minutes later, I'm sitting in a very crowded Cafe. They must be taking a break from their Christmas shopping. I'm sitting at a table by myself, cramped though it may be, with my laptop. Writing. I rarely order food when I go out, but I did this time. I didn't get a meal, technically, but it is still food, and even though it's lunch time, all I needed was a something small.

My fingers are hitting the keys on my keyboard at an extraordinary pace. I adjust my seating position, and I knock over the bag at my feet. I had decided to bring *Factory Street* with me to force some kind of inspiration. The inspiration hasn't come yet, but I felt that it was the thought that counted. *Factory Street* slides out of my bag and onto the floor. I lean down in exasperation and scoop it up, and stick it on the chair next to me. I wasn't expecting any visitors, or anyone to sit next to me and drool over my script like the last time I occupied this booth. Speaking of which...

Yep. There she is. On the other side of the restaurant, who should be sitting there, eating a sandwich, but Samantha I-don't-know-her-last-name. I zip up my bag, and place it on the ground under my chair, so that there's no chance of me knocking it over and her seeing it. When I look up, she's looking at me. She waves. I nonchalantly wave back. I'm not really interested in having a conversation with her. I've been doing so well not thinking about her, but I already know she intends to walk over here and join me. I type one last sentence in my story before Sam has put her food on the table, and moves the chair so she can sit down.

"Well, hi there," she greets me enthusiastically.

"Hey," I reply, wondering how long it will take her to ask me about *Factory Street*.

"How's the writing coming? I assume that's what you're doing."

"I'm actually making a website that allows people to see what kind of person their neighbor is."

"Oh really?" She seems interested in this false concept.

"No. I'm writing a new story to pass the time. I've been doing it all week," I say.

"Ooh, that sounds like fun. What's it about?" she asks.

"It's something of a murder mystery," I answer.

"I like those. Tell me more."

I chuckle. "Not this time. It's far from finished." I hope she'll drop the subject. But something in me tells me that she's not going to forget.

"Fine," Sam says, clearly let down, but she bounces back quickly.

"What are you doing tomorrow, it being Christmas and all? Do you see family?"

Another subject I'm not keen on discussing.

"Actually, my Christmas plans involve me eating, writing, relaxing, the movies, and going to bed."

"Aw, that's sad," Sam responds, frowning.

It sounds amazing to me.

"Not really. I have no intention of spending Christmas with my family." I shift my position in my seat, and continue. "Staying in my apartment on the twenty-fifth is preferred to visiting my family."

Sam tilts her head slightly, a bewildered look on her face.

"Really? I love seeing my family. This year I'm just see my friends from work. Can't imagine spending Christmas by myself. I mean, clearly I'm not seeing the big picture here. Even if you don't really get along with your family, can't you tolerate one day with them?"

"Nope," I say. "It's awkward even being in their presence. They're all just an overload of embarrassment, and they have a tendency to make me want to become a monk."

Sam raises an eyebrow.

"Okay, fine," I admit. "Maybe not a monk."

She smiles.

"I'm leaning towards hermit."

She laughs again. At least she thinks I'm funny. We sit in silence for a minute or two, watching the customers order their food, eat, and leave. Samantha turns to look at me. She's smiling again.

"Well," she starts. "I'll just have to see what I can do to make you have a good Christmas. But not right now, obviously: I have to do some last minute gift shopping." She stands up and pushes in her chair. "Just be ready by noon tomorrow, okay? I'll be dropping by."

She walks away before I have the chance to respond. Great. Should I buy a gift for Samantha? No. Maybe. I'll figure it out. Yes. No. I close the lid to my laptop, throw away my trash, and leave. Sam is across the street, climbing into a car. No matter what I decide to do next, I should put my laptop back in my apartment. It's good that I'm so observant and level-headed.

I open my apartment door to find my living space as simple and clean as ever. Nothing exciting happening, just peace. Plain, acceptable peace.

My night is quiet. Long and quiet. Four in the morning and I'm still lying awake, staring with an empty gaze at my blank ceiling. My brain sends a signal into itself, trying to figure out what's keeping me conscious for so long. If I don't fall asleep soon, I'll sleep through Christmas.

The signal returns with no useful information so I climb out of bed. I discover my leg is asleep as I pick myself off the floor, and start to navigate to the kitchen where I pour myself a glass of milk. I've heard of warm milk being very good for helping you sleep, but I've never tried it. It sounds disgusting.

I sigh and close my eyes as I lean on the counter.

I open my eyes, and although I am staring at my ceiling, it's not the ceiling above my bed, but rather the ceiling in my kitchen. Someone knocks on my door.

I sit up, looking around. There's a glass, surrounded by a pool of milk, lying on the floor next to me. A few seconds pass.

My door knocks again.

"No one's home," I say.

"Very funny," says the voice on the other side of the door. It's Samantha. I suppose I should let her in. I swing the door open, catching it before it hits the wall. Samantha's hair is tied up in a ponytail, and the bottom of a very blue dress trails out of her winter coat.

She looks... seraphic. She looks like a girl that any writer would spend nights writing about. Because a girl like her would keep him awake, clawing at the inside of his skull, itching to be free of his mind.

"Well, I had expected you to be up by now. And dressed," she says, her eyes searching me in all my under-dressed glory.

I look at the clock. It's quarter after twelve. I'm still in my pajamas.

"You're late," I say. A weak attempt to deflect the conversation from my own appearance. I'm thinking it will fail.

"So are you," Sam responds. "And you're not dressed."

"I'm well aware of how I am dressed. I might not have had the perfect night's sleep, which is why I woke up late."

She probably thinks I'm crazy. Sam gives me a look. Yeah, she thinks I'm crazy.

"However," I continue, "if you'll give me a few moments I can put on some proper clothes and I'll be ready. If you'd kindly wait in the living room?"

"All right," Sam says. "I suppose I can live with that."

"Thank you," I reply, and she heads for my comfiest chair. I leave the kitchen, go to my bedroom and open my closet. I can hear Sam walk around, most likely exploring my apartment.

Finally dressed, I return to my living room. Sam is standing by my bookcases. She notices me, and turns around.

"I notice you're a fan of Leonard."

"One could say that," I answer. "I'm in the middle of his books."

"Which one?" she asks.

"All of them," I say.

She looks puzzled.

"I don't think there's any way I could keep track of all of these," she says, turning to and gesturing at the bookcases.

She looks back at me.

"Well," she says, "shall we go?"

"Absolutely," I respond, and I walk to the door and

open it. Sam walks through and I lock the door behind me.

After an hour I'm pulling into the driveway of a one-story monstrosity. It must be at least sixty feet wide, and a hundred and fifty feet long, with the door planted in the middle. The house has a very large front lawn to go with the driveway. Maybe the owner of this house is an author she wants me to meet. Maybe. Or maybe I'm still tired.

As Sam knocks on the door she explains, "This is my friend Mark's house. He's very nice, so do your best to put up with him."

The door is opened by a man who looks about my age, wearing a bright red sweater with an elf on it, and a Santa hat.

"Sam!" They hug each other.

"Hi, Mark," she says, smiling. Already I'm out of place.

Hugs.

"This is Derek. He's a writer," Sam says. I give a small smile, and I shake Mark's hand.

"Oh dude that's awesome!" Mark says. He's overly enthusiastic. Or maybe he's just never seen a human before.

"I'm a director myself. No work without you guys," he smiles as he talks. I smile a little wider, and force a small laugh.

Ha.

Mark steps aside to let us into his house, and I follow Sam. It's as if someone had a wall, and forgotten to put in a door, so they knocked a large hole in it post-construction. There's a wide hallway extending out in front of me, with large rooms on either side. The rooms are packed with people, almost all of them holding dark brown bottles.

Mark thrusts a bottle into my own hand, says "Enjoy," and walks away. I deposit my beer into the hands of a thirsty individual whose slurred vocabulary is already difficult to understand. Sam had taken a quick drink from her bottle, so I doubt she intends to get rid of hers. I look around once more, and Sam's gone. I sigh, and start looking for a seat.

Five minutes later and I have indeed found a seat. It's actually a pair of seats, which might prove useful if Samantha reappears. I sit there in silence, observing the people that I want nothing to do with, and soon Mark comes and sits next to me.

"So tell me," he starts. "What do you write? Books, short stories, scripts?"

I guess I might as well talk to him.

"Scripts. I'm a playwright."

"Ever thought about writing for the movies?" Mark asks.

"Not really. Never intended for anyone else to read them, or act them out."

"So why write them?"

"When I started, I thought hardly anyone writes plays anymore, so I thought I'd write some. Then I became attached to the style."

"How many have you written?"

"Over the years, I'd say about seven or eight."

"Good amount," Mark says. He's still enthusiastic. "What do you write about?"

"The complexities of man and how he deals with age."

"Are you writing anything currently?" he asks.

"Actually yes, but I'm keeping it under wraps for now. I'd like to make more progress before I talk about it."

"Usually a good move," Mark agrees with me. At least there's that about him, but I'm still not interested in talking to him. I wish Sam would show up so that I wouldn't have to deal with him by myself. She could act as a buffer between us, and she can do all the talking.

And then here's Sam, appearing out of nowhere.

"Why, hello again," Mark says, rising to greet Sam again.

"Hello to you too, sir." Sam sits down in Mark's seat, cutting him off from any sort of convenience in talking to me at all.

"Well, I must be going," he says, looking around awkwardly.

Good.

And Mark walks away once more.

"What'd you think of him?" Sam asks me.

"I was counting the seconds."

"That's rude of you," she says.

"He's just not my type of person."

"What is your type of person?"

"Not him," I say.

"That's even worse," Sam says, laughing.

"So where were you?" I ask, changing the subject.

"Avoiding someone."

She averts her eyes, not looking at me.

"Are you okay?"

"Of course, why wouldn't I be?" she asks.

"The fact that you've spent this party avoiding someone."

I raise an eyebrow. She still doesn't look at me.

"Fine," I start. "If you can tell me you're okay, and look me in the eye while doing it, then I'll drop it."

She looks at me, and a split second later she looks away again.

"Okay, so I'm not in the greatest condition. I just didn't want to show up here by myself."

She looks at me and says, "Mark's roommate is kind of an ex-boyfriend."

I nod my head.

"Ah," I say.

"Yeah."

"So why show up today at all?" I wonder.

"Because I'm still friends with Mark, and there was a chance of *him* not being here. But we showed up, and he was one of the first ones that I saw. So I ducked away."

"And left me by myself," I finish.

"I'm sorry," Sam says, tears shining in her eyes, with true apology.

"It's fine."

It really is. I'm not upset at Sam. Just very curious.

"Do you want to leave?" I ask, hoping this is a considerate question.

She doesn't answer. She just looks around the room, glancing at different people.

"What's on your mind?" I think maybe a different question might get a response out of her.

"Him," she speaks quietly. I have to strain to hear. She continues. "Malcolm. I met him when I first came here. Not exactly the nicest guy. It was a huge mistake. Everything with him just went too far. I took off one day, and I just left. I blocked his number. And then Mark calls me, tells me about this party, and that he'd understand if I didn't want to come. So here I am. I guess I was hoping that it wouldn't bother me to see him again. And you know, I'm not sure, at all, why I'm here now."

I don't know what to say...

"The bruises faded after a while, so I guess I'm really okay."

Sam's voice wavers as she finishes talking, and she looks at the floor. I have no idea what to say. No one's ever opened up to me like this. No one's ever told me a secret so large. I've written about this in a script or two, but I controlled those situations. But here she is, telling me she'd been abused by someone she trusted. I don't even know where to start. I should probably figure out a response soon. Or let her keep going. I should say something, but she speaks first.

"Have you ever been with someone you wanted to leave, but felt you couldn't?"

She looks up at me, and I stare at her.

"No," I say, unsure how to follow up my short answer.

I'm clueless. This is a totally different area of thinking, and conversation, and communication in general. I think back to a script, and an idea floats to the front of my brain. Yes, I could try that. I lift my arm up and put it around Samantha's shoulders. Her reaction is almost immediate. At my touch she leans in, letting her weight fall into me. Her shoulders fit snugly within my one-winged embrace.

Something hits my knee, and I look down. There's a single dark spot, almost perfectly round, on my leg. A tear. She's crying, and sadness hits me. It pains me to see her like this. On Christmas, too. This isn't right. I pull her tighter to me, and I pull her tighter, doing my paltry best to make her feel better. A light bulb comes on above my head. Convenience. I can fix this.

I stand up and take her by the hand. She looks up at me, and I smile. She wipes the tears from her face, and stands up as well. I lead her out of the house, and I help her into my car.

Neither of us speak as I drive. I can only imagine what's going on in her head.

After forty minutes or so, I stop the car. I shut off the engine, but leave the headlights shining forward, into the blackness. Ahead of us is what some might call a cliff.

A cliff with a bench. There are at least two inches of snow all around us, covering everything. I look at Sam, who seems intrigued. She wipes one last tear from her eye, and she looks back. Something large moves in the backseat, and we both jump.

"Whass-goin-on?" a slurred voice says.

A stranger is sitting in my backseat, clearly intoxicated, and clueless.

"Well," I begin, "we are currently overlooking the city, and you, a nameless person, are illegally in my car."

"Now you know!" the man says back, even more slurred than before.

Sam lets out a sigh. She looks even sadder than she did when we were at the party. I need to do something.

"Wait here," I say to the man in the back seat. "I'll deal with you later. Try not to disrupt anything, or... vomit. I like it clean in here."

The stranger responds by quickly descending into my backseat. I get out of the car, rush around the front and help Sam climb out of the passenger seat. I lead her forward to the bench, and after brushing off the snow, I invite her to sit next to me.

Personally, I think the city looks amazing. Especially at night. The web of lights, coming from street lamps, car headlights, and the lamps in the windows of the night-owls who spend the dark hours working as their loved ones and neighbors sleep.

"This was my favorite place to go as a child," I say, breaking the silence.

Sam looks up, her eyes starting to droop. She's getting tired.

"Yeah. I found this place with my Dad by accident when I was ten years old. My parents had always wanted me to be a more outdoorsy type of kid, so one day Dad took my brother and I out in the car, and we drove around for over an hour. I think Dad was trying to confuse us with the driving time."

Samantha's eyes continue to droop, though by the slight smile and nod she gives, she's still listening.

"It had been raining all day, so by the time he drove up here, the hill was muddy and he had to really press on the gas pedal to get us up here. Of course, he pressed on it so hard that we shot up, and crashed into a rock. That rock, actually," and I pointed to a boulder that had no sign it had ever been hit by a car.

"That was a long day. I spent it sitting on the edge of the cliff. After that day, and up until the day I left home, I'd come here as often as I could, and just sit. My Dad built this bench. He realized that I wasn't a kid that was going to play outside, or be a social butterfly. By the fourth time I had asked to be driven up here, he'd made this bench. Dad always understood me, but Mom was just so over the top, Dad kinda faded into the background. You'd never have known he was a man who cared about anything more than football."

Sam's eyes are now more open than they were before. That's a good sign. Now is as good a time as any to take her home.

"Come on," I said, taking her by the hands and helping her to her feet. "It's time to go."

She's awake, but drowsy. I wonder if she's going to remember my childhood memory tomorrow. I help Sam back into my car, and close the door behind her. Climbing into the driver's seat once more, I shut that door.

"Are you two lovebirds -*hic*- ready to go now?" comes the drunken voice from the back. "I'm freezing my tail off, and your -*hic*- lumpy seats are far from luxuri-*hic*-ous," he hiccuped.

"We're ready," I answered, and turn the key.

CHAPTER EIGHT

It's nine in the morning. My phone is ringing. I'm in bed. My phone is on the floor. I'm in bed. I *was* sleeping. My brain hasn't started to wake itself up yet. I'm in no mood, or condition, to answer the phone. I let it ring. It doesn't stop ringing. A groan escapes my mouth, and I flop out of bed onto the floor, but when I reach my phone it stops ringing. In the silence I hear another noise. The shower. My shower is on. Why is my shower on? I stand up and walk towards the bathroom door, and I hear another sound. Singing. A man is singing opera in my shower. I knock on the door. The voice stops singing, and responds.

"I'll be out in five minutes Derek!"

Greg's in the shower. For a second I forget he lives here. The shower turns off, and Greg resumes his operatic singing. Greg is a thirty-year-old man with short, blond hair that seems almost permanently unkempt from the lack of showering. When Greg broke into my car nearly a month ago, he fell asleep in my backseat after a severe drinking marathon because his girlfriend of three years had left him. I had half-carried and half-dragged him into my apartment, and Sam convinced me to let him sleep on my couch for the night. The following morning I woke him up, and he told me his story.

He'd been a slacker from a wealthy family and when he met Lucy his life changed... for about a year. He backslid and stopped being serious about life and repeatedly put himself in situations that would get him in trouble. Lucy put up with it for only so long. Although he lost Lucy, he kept his money. Greg's family owns a prestigious oil company, so he's well off. After Greg told me his story, we made a deal. Greg would pay me to live in my apartment (a very, *very* large amount of money, I might add), and I would do what I can to help him get over Lucy. I needed the money, and there was a chance this would help me become more sociable. Greg has made a lot of progress in the last month; I have not been nearly as successful as he.

Greg walks through the living room, into the kitchen, wearing only a towel around his waist.

"Oh come on," I say, shielding my eyes and looking away. "Have some decency will you?"

"It's just me, man," he responds, bending over to peer into the fridge. "There are going to be instances when this is absolutely necessary."

"Is this one of those times?" I ask.

"No. This is preparation for the necessary. Is your girlfriend coming over today?"

Don't worry, it's not true. Sam is not my girlfriend.

"She's not my girlfriend," I clarify.

Greg laughs. "Dude, I've been living here for a month, and she's been here more times than I have."

"Absolutely untrue," I say, trying to conceal a smile.

Greg turns to look at me and holds up his fingers to count.

"She was here Monday because she went shopping for us, Tuesday because we watched a movie-"

"That was all you," I interject.

"Wednesday... she wasn't here," he pauses.

"Told you," I say.

"But she was here yesterday to help you fix the garbage disposal."

"And you weren't home," I say.

"Then you should have waited," he says. He turns his attention back to the fridge and grabs food left and right.

Sam does stop by often. Since I had given her a copy of *Factory Street*, she had developed a habit of coming by a few times a week to discuss the play.

Greg finishes getting his snack and returns to the bathroom.

"You'd better throw that trash away when you're done!" I called after him.

Greg grunts in reply, his mouth full of apple. Don't get me wrong, I enjoy Greg's company. He adds interest to my day. I haven't felt a need to attend a funeral since he's been here. The near-constant company of a human being like Greg has done something. I don't know exactly what, but in helping him, he's helped me with more than just my rent.

Greg returns to the Living Room, and stands before me.

"I forgot to mention," he says, "We've got plans. I hope you don't mind."

He just looks at me. And I look at him.

Twenty minutes later, I'm laying flat on the ice staring up at Greg's face as he looks down at me, a smile wide on his face.

"When you said you had never been ice skating before, I thought you were kidding," Greg says, as he helps me back up.

"When you said you had made plans to go ice skating, I knew you were serious, but I didn't think I had to be there!"

Greg's smile doesn't falter. At least he thinks I'm funny. He pats me on the back, and says, "Catch up!"

I don't skate.

I turn around, slip, and try to regain my balance. If I ever catch up to Greg, I'm going to kill him, bring him back to life, and bury him.

The ice rink isn't crowded. It's Wednesday morning.

The occupants are Greg, myself, and three other adults. Two men, one woman. We count how many times I wind up flopping onto the ice, to Greg's delight. As I cling to the wall surrounding the ice, I hide my smile from Greg. I'm dead set on him not knowing that I'm starting to enjoy myself. I look up, and he's skating towards me. As he comes closer I push away from the wall, sailing towards him, and he crashes into me.

"Maybe we should start counting your falls," I say, again laying on the ice. Neither of us attempt to get up.

"Maybe we should just go home now," Greg's voice comes from somewhere to my left.

Upon arriving back at our apartment, there is a note on my door. I recognize Sam's elegant handwriting that reads "Greg and Derek: Dinner. Tonight. 7 PM. 'No' is not an acceptable answer."

"Looks like we're going out tonight!" Greg says enthusiastically, clapping me on the back. I've been getting way too much fresh air for a writer.

We go inside, and Greg puts on a movie while I get some lunch. Greg has taken it upon himself to introduce me to a great many new bands and movies. Helping me appreciate the fact that I write scripts, he's been showing me his favorite movies which, in his mind, have the greatest writing of all time. I won't say which films I agree with him on. In the month he's been living here, we've had to go out and buy an extra bookcase to hold the Blu-Ray's and DVD's and rare VHS tapes that Greg buys for us to watch. We've even established a movie night.

Greg's something of a film enthusiast, and uses that enthusiasm to run a blog where he critiques the movies he watches. He's pretty popular on the internet, and has quite a following. Every now and then, a famous magazine asks for his opinions on various topics. We pass the time this afternoon watching the movie, and when it's over start to get ready for our dinner.

As a tradeoff, I've introduced Greg to wearing suits, and he now takes every opportunity wear them, so when we arrive at the restaurant, we both look presentable.

Since it's a Wednesday night, it's not very busy, so we don't have much of a wait to be seated. Greg tells the woman serving us his name, and that we're waiting for a third- a woman. The waitress tells him that Sam is already seated and waiting for us. Sam stands up to greet and hug us, and we sit down. Greg and Sam on one side, and myself on the other.

Sam is wearing casual clothes. Long sleeved shirt, with jeans, but I decide not to say anything about it.

I haven't eaten out with someone else like this since the so-called Massacre of Noodles in 2009. A snide comment concerning myself and some alcohol and/or drugs by my brother resulted in an over-enthusiastic great-aunt of mine pulling out a small pistol from her purse, and attempting to shoot him or myself from across the room. It happened pretty fast, so the memory is a little fuzzy.

I haven't been invited to an extended family dinner since.

I've kept to myself, and aside from the instances where a certain female has somehow found me eating at restaurants that I frequent, I eat out all by my lonesome. I like it that way, but I do also enjoy spending time with Sam and Greg.

Greg orders a Sprite, Sam orders a glass of water, no lemon, and I order a Coke. No one says anything after the waitress leaves to give us time to decide on our order. Greg speaks up first.

"Derek went ice skating today," he stated, as though this were an offhand thought. "He looked very pretty, flying into the walls and falling onto the ice."

Greg smirks, and Sam chuckles.

"Way to go," Sam says. I look up from my menu, pulling my attention away.

"And you looked gorgeous in your skirt. Pink is definitely your color," I say, also smiling, Sam and Greg are both laughing now. "In all seriousness," I continue, "it was pretty fun. I'm not gonna rush to do it again. I like being able to stand up properly."

"That's very understandable. I'm not really a fan of it either," says Sam.

The waitress comes by with our drinks, and we thank her. She asks if we're ready to order. We say not yet.

"I'll come back in a few minutes then!" the waitress says with a smile, and she's gone.

"I'm feeling the steak," I say.

"Same here," Greg agrees.

Sam looks at the two of us. "Boys." Greg shrugs, and he and I close our menus.

"Well, I'm going with the Quesadillas. Because I'm feeling that," Sam says, also closing her menu.

The waitress returns, and takes our orders. She walks away once more. Same turns to look at Greg.

"Have you seen any movies lately?"

"Of course," Greg says. "Have you known me to do anything else?"

I've yet to mention that, hidden underneath Greg's unkempt appearance, is a voice that can go from neutral to sarcastic in a split-second. It keeps me entertained.

"Point taken," Sam continues. "So answer the question! What have you seen?"

Greg smiles. "Well," he pauses. "First I'd have to remember. I've seen a lot of movies in the last few days."

"We watched *Arrogant Conqueror* last night," I say.

"Yes. Yes we did."

"Well?" Sam says. "What'd you think?" Sam was the one who recommended we watch it in the first place, as it has her favorite actor in it, and she thinks the writing is like my own. In fact, she thought I had written it. This turned out to not be true.

"There was too little story, and too much carnage," Greg says. "Violence without a purpose is not as attractive as some think. There's a difference between directors like Aranas and Faultine. Most people prefer Faultine, and even more people prefer Spielberg to either. Substance over style."

I see our food coming from the kitchen and I immediately stop paying attention to either of them. It's set at our places, and as I look back up at them I remember that we were in the middle of a conversation.

"But that's not the point!" Sam is saying.

"Yes it is."

"No it's not," she says.

"Just because you thought his writing was similar, doesn't mean it had good writing," says Greg.

"Don't you think that's a little insulting to his writing?" asks Sam.

"I think what you said was insulting to his writing."

Ohh. They're talking about the comparison in my writing and the writing behind *Arrogant*. This is starting to make more sense.

"Might I interject?" I ask.

"No!" Sam and Greg spoke in unison. They return to debating, and I start to eat my food before it gets cold. My steak is perfect.

"...because you think Hot Pockets are one of the four food group—"

Sam stops talking mid-sentence. I look up, and she's staring across the restaurant. I follow her gaze.

"Time to go," I say.

"What's wrong with you guys?" Greg asks, looking at his food like he'll never get the chance to eat again.

Lucy is sitting three tables away, with another man. Sam throws some money on the table, and we grab Greg by the arms and march him out of the restaurant, and luckily he doesn't see her until we're out the door.

We sit in my car. Sam in the front seat, Greg and I in the back. We lock the doors.

"Why did you take me out of there?" Greg asks, his voice shaking with anger. The first thing that pops into my head is how much he's wrinkling that suit.

"You can't be there." I'm hoping I said that with enough force to be convincing. Sam eases out of the parking space, and starts driving.

"Says you," says Greg.

"Says the guy who's your mentor," I reply.

"Says the guy who's so socially deformed he can't even face his family, and whose only job was to get me over her..." He stops, and looks down at his lap. "Maybe I'm not ready."

"No, you're not," I say. "I know more about you than you do. More than you've ever told me."

"Like what?"

"Like the fact that you're an orphan."

No one says anything.

It just slipped out. I hadn't meant to say it, but I did. We're not even moving anymore. We're already at our building.

"I can read you like an open book. If you had said anything to her, it would have wound up with you getting angry at each other and even though it's not my money, I have no intention of bailing you out of prison for disturbing the peace!" I finish. Greg stares. He seems to be calming down. He opens the door and gets out of the car, and closes the door behind him. As I watch him walk into our building I look at Sam.

"We left your car at the restaurant."

"Nope. I walked from home."

"Oh, okay," I say.

"Should I stay here?" she asks. "If something goes wrong maybe a second person should be there too."

"Yeah, sure. Greg seems like he could use another person around."

By the time we walk through the door, Greg is already in his room with the door closed. I give Sam some pajamas that I think will fit her comfortably, and I turn the couch into the fold-out bed it knew it always was, though I've never had a use for it before now. I say good night to Sam, and retreat to my own bedroom. Laying on my back, staring at the ceiling, I try and will myself to sleep. Hopefully I'll dream of a way to deal with this in the morning.

I wake up. I look at my clock and discover that it's quarter after nine in the morning. I put on a robe and leave my bedroom. In the main room, I see Samantha sitting at the table, reading a book. She's dressed in her clothes from the night before.

My phone starts ringing from the other room. I go in to look and find it on the floor. It's my Mom.

"Hello?" I answer.

"Hi Derek." I can hear the sadness laced in the two words. "Sweetie, I'm afraid I have some bad news."

My brain goes blank and my ears create a fog that prevents me from processing the worst words I've ever heard. Words that make me cringe and fall to my knees.

"Can you– Can you say that again?" I say as my head falls. A tear falls down my cheek.

"I said your father died last night," my Mother says again, and I can almost hear the tears in her words. "I can understand if you don't want to come by, but we'd really appreciate it..."

More tears.

"...the viewing is on Friday, and the funeral is on Saturday."

Another cloud seems to cover my ears. It feels like forever has passed without me properly listening, though I've heard every horrifying word.

"Are you okay, Derek?" my Mother asks. "Sweetheart?"

I say that I'm fine, and hang up the phone and let it fall to the floor. I look up and through my glazed eyes see Sam and Greg both standing in the doorway. I stand up, wiping tears from my eyes, and before I even make it to the bathroom, I collapse onto the floor. From a distance I hear my name being said in worried tones, but I can't tell who's speaking.

I just want to sleep. The darkness gets closer, and I want so badly to give in— to remain motionless. In the end we are all going, but that doesn't mean that I'm willing to experience it now. My eyelids have closed.

As the over-extending blanket of darkness surrounds me, the voices of the last remaining foundation fade away.

We are all going.

CHAPTER NINE

I originally hadn't intended to go to the viewing. To willingly spend time with members of my extended family who thought of me as an alcoholic and possible drug addict, and who had at one point tried to lure me to a psych ward to check me in, was not an attractive prospect. But...

The one solid foundation in my life was my father. Gone. Forever. All he is now is a cold lifeless corpse, like a porcelain replica, his body on display for the room to see, and we'll sob over him in a cold desperation that one can only hope and pray will end soon.

Sam and Greg are here with me. They decided they wanted to see my Father, and they could run interference and block unwanted family members from reaching me. I'm standing in front of my Father, seeing his face for the final time. He's wearing a suit, with faded places from years of use. My Father, like myself, is a suit man. Was a suit man. He found something to do at church on a near daily basis, and I had attended with him until the day I moved out. My Father was the only person to let me know that love existed. My Mother gave birth to me, but my Father gave me life. Sam mutters something about needing some air, and Greg grunts. They leave me standing next to my Father.

I've never been closer to death than now. In all the funerals, and all the weeping families, it's never been personal for me. There's no one to talk to. There's nothing to learn. I know my Father as well as I ever will. I'm the family here. I'm the story-teller. I'm the grieving victim, deprived of a soul that has departed this earth and gone to join our Heavenly Father.

"Hi Derek."

I turn to see Marshall. I look around, and notice that not only are we alone, but there are fifteen clear feet of standing room. I guess my family knows I'm here.

"Hi. Where's the wife and kids?" I ask. We look at our Father.

"Gone."

"Gone?"

"As in two weeks ago Kelly packed her bags, grabbed the kids, and left."

"Oh," I say. "I'm sorry."

"I think she started packing when she realized she had spent almost all of my money. But you know what?" Marshall says, tilting his head towards me. "I'm glad it happened. Don't get me wrong, I miss my kids. I haven't heard from them since. But Kelly..."

Marshall utters some unsavory adjectives about his wife. He takes a few breaths.

"I'm not sorry she's gone," he says after a moment. "I mean, you saw her for what she was."

I nod.

"I'm not sorry she's gone," Marshall says again..

"Me neither," I say, and Marshall smiles.

"What's your favorite memory of him?" he asks, and my own smile starts to fade as I think.

What was my favorite memory? What memories could I retrieve? And it hits me.

"When I was fifteen years old, he found my first script lying on the floor in the kitchen. You had called me some name, and got on my case for being uncool and trying to write. He stumbled upon the aftermath. He read my script, and came to my room. I was crying..."

I pause for a moment, catching my breath, collecting my thoughts, swallowing hard.

"... He came and told me that he loved it. That script

was about him. It was about adventures we would have. That car trip we took was in there. I embellished a lot, of course, but the basics were still there. The script was terrible. But he told me he loved it all the same."

Marshall turns to look at me and we hug.

"I'll deal with Mom," he says into my ear. "You go home. Get some sleep, and I'll see you tomorrow. Okay?"

I nod. We part, and I turn to my Father —my Dad— one last time.

"I miss you Dad."

As I turn to walk towards the door, I see Sam and Greg standing just inside the room. They're smiling. I wipe the tears from my face, and I walk out of the room, the two trailing behind me. Greg drives, and Sam sits next to me in the back seat. Greg and I haven't spoken about the other night, and we haven't needed to. We have something of an unspoken agreement.

If I can take one sentence to address something startling: my brother is a person. A fully legitimate, and likable, person.

Sam puts her hand on mine, and squeezes.

...And that's a feeling I haven't had in a while. I've been attempting to banish the idea of having feelings for this woman since the first dream.

**

The morning of the funeral I wear my darkest suit. The service is quiet. The soft sobbing echoes inside the church. My pastor nods a hello to me. Though I attend often, I do not speak with my pastor. He is a distant individual. As far as pastors go, I'm not sure if pastor is an appropriate title for him. To my knowledge he does little else than stand in front of his audience on Sunday mornings and speak for an hour, before returning to his real life as a recluse. He once said his reason for seclusion is that he had seen enough of the world, not to depart, but to live apart.

I'm polite, and nod back. After fifteen minutes people are still filing in when the pastor stands up.

"Donald Wilson. The man who inspired..."

Though this is about my Father, I'm not very interested in what this man has to say. He knows nothing about any of us. He knows as much about my Father as he does about being a pastor— astonishingly little. My pastor doesn't speak for long, and he says my name, motioning for me to come forward.

I stand up, and make my way to the front of the church. The entire church is silent, my footsteps breaking the quiet. Even some of my relatives have stifled their sobs to glare at me. I let my fingertips graze the coffin as I walk by. I turn to face the congregation when I arrive at the pulpit. Sam and Greg enter the church at this moment. They sit in the back, exactly next to where I had been seated. I clear my throat, and I open my mouth. No words come out. I clear my throat again.

"My Father," I begin, and a lump catches in my throat.

"My Father," I start again, "is the reason I'm here. And the reason all of you are here. Whether you knew him as Donald, or Mr. Wilson, this man was a rock. My Father. He was the only thing that kept me going for my entirety life. He is the reason I ever knew that there is, and was, a God. That just because your life isn't going the way you want it to, God will put something, or in my case, someone, in your life to keep you upright and walking, even after you've stumbled off the path entirely. My Father raised me, and-" out of the corner I see my Mother looking offended. "-he's the one who taught me everything I know now. The majority of my family members, both near and far, did what they could to shut me out. Over the years I've been called a drunkard, a drug-dealer, a misogynist, a terrorist, and one particular individual said I deserved to have been aborted. I've been asked how AA was going for me... By my *family*.

"But my Father... my Dad. My Dad told me he loved me. My Dad told me that I was worthwhile. My Dad told me that there was nothing wrong with writing. My Dad spent time with me. My Dad showed me the Grace of God, and up until recently, it was only my Dad who showed me compassion."

I can see my brother smiling from the corner of my eye.

"My Dad was more of a man than I could ever hope to be. And I pray that even a fraction of his personality is left behind in those who knew him."

And with that I step down from behind the pulpit, and I walk back to my seat. Then Marshall is sitting with the three of us. Ten minutes later the pallbearers carry Dad's body out to the hearse, and we're off in our motorcade of sorrow. The ride to the cemetery is short, and in mere minutes we're all standing by the grave, which is surrounded by flowers, and the pastor says a prayer.

Marshall steps forward, and says a goodbye. I follow suit. The cold wind hits my face and forces a tear down my face in a crude, zig-zag line. I lean over the grave, and the tear lands on the coffin.

Lastly is Mom. Honestly, I don't have anything to say to her, and even if I did, I don't think she wants to hear from me. Before I turn to leave, I look at Dad's coffin once more. Thank God for true men like him. Greg pats me on the back, and we walk away. Marshall nods towards me. Unspoken agreement. I nod back. Marshall puts his arm around Mom, and they're out of my vision.

The car ride back to my apartment is silent for the most part. Sam says it was a nice service. At least what I said was nice, she says. Greg tells me that I did a good job.

"When did you write that?" Sam asks me.

"I didn't," I say.

"So you just-"

"I winged it, yeah."

"Wow," says Greg.

"I do that sometimes," I say.

"It helps that you're good at it," Sam says.

"Thanks."

My brain is ready to slow down. Greg says that sleep is a good idea. We could all use some sleep.

**

I haven't seen Sam in the two days since the funeral, but I live with Greg, so I see him plenty. In fact, he came up to the roof of the building with me, as neither of us could sleep.

In a week where my Dad died and Greg saw his ex on a date with another man, it's nice to escape and enjoy looking at the stars in the cold blueness of twenty-eight degree weather.

Greg keeps a lawn chair on the roof. When Greg wants time to himself, or wants to read, he comes up here. I got a second lawn chair for tonight's sleepless festivities.

"Have you ever been in love?" Greg asks.

"Maybe. Sometimes it's hard to tell."

"I know exactly what you mean," he says

"What do *you* mean, though?" I wonder.

"I mean have you ever thought about, not seen and then thought, I mean simply thought about a girl and been filled with so much frustration and joy that you loved her, but you weren't with her?"

"I don't think so," I say.

"It's a weird feeling. Like you have one sole purpose, and it's to do everything possible for that person. Doesn't matter what it is, but if it makes them happy, you wanna do it."

"I think there's something wrong with your drink."

"I'm serious," Greg frowns.

"I know, I'm kidding," I say.

"That's what it was like at first," he says. "Like nothing else mattered. But then life resumes. Being with someone so long— there were times when I really wanted to try, but it was so fleeting." He pauses and looks at me. "Being in a long-term relationship doesn't change you. It reveals you."

I nod, and look back up at the sky.

"How would you say I'm doing, so far?" Greg asks.

"Can I decide in the daytime when I'm not staring into the stars?" I say. "For the record though, you're getting there."

"Even with everything," he says, "life is starting to make sense again, and I like it."

"I'll think about that more tomorrow," I answer.

I finally finish my drink, and Greg produces a pack of chocolate chip cookies.

"You sly dog."

He smiles and says, "They were a gift from Sam. To you, actually. Don't be mad, but I ate two earlier today."

Greg hands me the package, and I attempt to use my shivering fingers to pry a cookie from the packaging and pop it in my mouth.

It's time to sleep. Drinks and cookies under the stars. Greg decides to take a shower first in order to warm up before sleep, but I'm fine with just brushing my teeth, putting on pajamas, and jumping into bed.

As I drift off to sleep, I think about the days ahead, and I'm happy for the first time in what feels like weeks.

CHAPTER TEN

The room is nothing but white. White walls and ceiling. White floor. White chairs. White sofa. White table. I'm sitting in the middle of the sofa. I'm wearing white clothes. Looking outside the window, I can't see anything other than a bright light shining through. Even my shoes are white, but my hair is unkempt- the only contradiction in this room crafted from pure order. Although everything is white, it has a slight blur factor to it.

It can be quite nice to sit on a couch by yourself. But when your companion is the person you miss the most, it's irreplaceable.

"Hi, Dad."

And he turns to look at me, and smiles.

"Hey, Derek."

Dad never referred to me as though I were a child, even when I was a child, or when I was an adult, and acted like a child.

"How was your trip?" I ask of him.

"Slow," his smile broadens now, and I smile too.

"I've missed you," my smile cracking slightly, I'm sure enough for him to notice, but he seems unaware.

"I've missed you," he says. "It's been too long."

"I agree."

"I miss the days when we could have dinner without an argument break out," Dad says.

"I was thinking the same thing."

"I know."

"Funny how that works."

"So how are you here?" I ask.

"How should I know? This is your dream. Your rules. Your wishes."

"Fair enough, I think." My Father laughs at my confusion.

"Regardless of the circumstances of me being here at all, I have a question," he says.

"Feel free to ask, though I think you already know the answer," I say.

"I probably do, but I'd rather hear it from you."

We sit in silence for a moment, and he asks.

"What is going on with you and Sam?"

Whether it's because I think that way, or because my Dad is asking me, I knew that was going to be the question.

"I wish I knew." I say, "There really isn't an easy answer for that."

"Sure there is," Dad says, once again undermining any previous thought I'd had to the contrary. "All you need to do is figure out the intentions. Question one. How do you feel about her?"

"I really like her, Dad."

"Good! Now we're getting somewhere," he says, almost laughing the last words.

"Okay, so what's question two?" I ask.

"Question two is, what was the one thing I taught you about a romantic relationship with a woman?"

"It's for life or it's for nothing," I answer.

"Good. So start thinking about that," he says.

"Alright," I finally say.

He leans forward. "Now, you say you really like her. Why?"

"Why not?"

"Don't be smart with me," he says.

This couch is starting to get uncomfortable.

"She's wonderful. She treats me like a person. She's been there for me. She takes an interest in things that I do. She's sensible. She's just been the most truly wonderful person I've ever met."

"Anything else?" Dad asks.

"For instance, what?"

"For instance, anything, genius."

"She has the most beautiful smile I've ever seen."

"I don't believe you."

"Why not?" I ask.

"Because my smile is the most beautiful I've ever seen."

"You've been looking in the mirror too long," I say.

"Okay," Dad continues, smiling. "So you know the girl, and you know why you like her so much. Now all you have to do is—"

"Wake up!"

**

We round the corner and regain full speed, our footsteps pounding the floor, creating thunder I'm sure will cause our neighbors to call our Super... But we're too fast. No witnesses.

No witnesses means no phone calls asking why we were tearing up the floor with our soles. No witnesses means that this almost isn't worth the trouble. No witnesses means we're gonna need to go faster.

Greg passes me and is half a hallway length ahead before I round the next corner. My door—the finish line— is in sight. Sam is standing by, ready to open it and let us in. Greg stumbles, his feet traveling faster than the rest of him. As he hits the floor I catch up and with a leap soar over him, landing in my door way. I rest my back against the wall, and slide down to the floor. Greg stands up and Sam is moving her hand, ushering us into the room, away from the scene. Sam hands the pair of us tall glasses of water. I sip from mine in between gasps of air.

"Apartment races were an awesome idea," Greg says. "Though if you want us to do it again, you're gonna have to move down two floors, so that I won't have to run so far."

"Or you could get more exercise," Sam says, smiling at Greg's out-of-breathedness.

"Or you could move."

"Or you could just not whine because a guy wearing jeans beat you," I chime in. Greg throws an ice cube at me.

"You better pick that up."

Greg moans something about his legs merely taking a small break. I get up and stand by the counter. Greg stands up as well, clearly trying not to be shown up by my effort, and as he ambles out of the room towards my shower, he's muttering about craving pizza.

"I'll be back when my calves regain power!" is heard from the bedroom.

Sam and I are alone in the room. I refill my water, and take my seat again. She's still standing. There's a moment of silence, sprinting towards awkward tension. She moves towards the door.

"Well I should probably head out. Got to start working on plans to move upstairs by two floors. Maybe three."

"Hey," I say, deciding that now is as good a time as any. "Would you want to go grab some dinner this week?" Waiting just the split-second it takes for her to answer is heart-stopping.

"Yeah that'd be fun." She's smiling. Good sign. "Maybe Marshall could come too. I'd love to meet him."

And deflating.

"Yeah that would be totally cool." Did I just turn into a twelve year old? "I'll text him later."

She smiles.

"Okay."

She closes the door after herself. Am I an idiot? That was definitely the wrong way to ask her out. I can do better next time. I think. Unless, this is still the same time. This is still the same opportunity. I stand up, wrench open the door, and my legs move slower than I do.

"Samanth-"

As I hit the floor, she turns around, sees me, and bursts out laughing. This is helpful.

But she doesn't move. She remains standing in the middle of the hallway. The door across the hall opens up, and an elderly man appears in the doorway.

"What's going on?" a woman's voice comes from behind him.

"It's those people across the hall. Making a ruckus."

"This is not a ruckus," I say, struggling to stand up, and brushing myself off.

Sam, still laughing, asks me if I'm okay. looks a little confused now, and starts walking towards me. An elderly woman joins the man in the doorway. The man appears to realize what I'm doing. He smiles. Now would be an ideal time to continue my original train of thought.

"Sam," I say, and she's still walking closer. "What I meant by dinner, was more along the lines of-"

"A date?" Sam asks, and she stops walking.

"Yes," I say. "I was intending for it to be a date, with simply you and I. But before you say anything, let me just say this-"

I hurry the last sentence to keep her from speaking. It's difficult to read her expression. I can't tell if she's impressed, happy, or horrified. All the while I'm trying not to think about the elderly couple still standing in the doorway just looking at us. I continue.

"I can't begin to describe how beautiful you are. In the three months I've known you, since that poor girls' funeral, I've just been running into you nonstop by accident, and I'd like to keep running into you by accident, on purpose, and I'd be the happiest guy on the planet if you said yes, and please respond soon so that my heart can slow down, because I think, combined with all that running it may explode and I won't hear your answer."

She smiles. That's a good sign. Right?

She steps forward, closing the distance between us. I'm still aware of the ever-present couple across the hall.

CHAPTER ELEVEN

I'm back on the pure white couch with my Dad. I'm probably dreaming, though I haven't decided yet.

"So she said yes?" asks Dad.

"I assume so," I say.

"Didn't she say?" His eyebrows raised.

"No."

"What happened?" he asks.

"She smiled, and walked away. And then that old couple next door invited me for drinks."

"Well," he says, "I would also assume that she said yes, without saying yes."

"Can they do that?" I ask. "Girls, I mean."

"As if they have a license."

"Does it ever work?"

"It worked on you," he says.

"Right." I'm suspicious.

"And it worked on me."

"Did it?" I ask.

"It's what your Mother did to me. I told you about how I asked her out, right?"

"Nope," I say.

"Oh. Well, it was late Summer, Nineteen Eighty-Something."

"You don't know the year?" I ask, amused.

"No. *You* don't know the year."

"Touché."

"May I continue?" he asks.

"Of course."

"Thank you."

Dad clears his throat rather theatrically.

"OK, so it's the Summer of Nineteen Eighty-One. Your Mother worked at the local deli. Wait, no, that was my job. I cleaned the place. Every window, table, and tile on the floor. No so-called sandwich artistry for me. She worked at the theater down the street, and came into my place on her breaks. So one day, she comes in, and your mother is beautiful. I mean, every guy in the place does a double take, and has to pick his jaw up from off the floor. She was the girl *everybody* wanted to date. So she goes up to the line, orders this sandwich, and waits. And I wait. Until she gets her sandwich, and I walk up to her. She stops when she sees me, and I say- 'Would you like to see a movie with me sometime?' Then she laughs, and walks away. The next day, I get a phone call from her, asking me when I'm gonna pick her up.

"So yes. I'd say there's a good chance she said yes."

And he's gone.

Sitting at a table with Sam and Greg I look up from my almost empty glass and see a No Smoking sign, and directly below the sign is a man lighting a cigarette. Amused, I wait for the management to come and yell at him. When they finally do, I'm very much let down. They simply ask him to leave. No shouting matches arising from the customer because he's too upset to listen. I feel cheated.

Sam's been talking for the last five minutes, with no response from me. Although Greg has been paying attention, so at least she has that. I think she's talking about coffee. As a non-coffee drinker, I believe I am entitled to not care.

Sam is sitting next to me, despite the fact that since our hallway interaction nearly three days ago we haven't said anything more than hello/goodbye earlier today. In all honesty though, Greg has been doing more than enough talking for all of us. He's a happy individual.

"So," Greg says. "I met someone."

"Who?" Sam asks, shifting eagerly in her seat.

"What's her name?" I ask.

"Her name is Hayley," Greg says, not even trying to conceal his smile.

"And where did you meet this Hayley?" Sam asks.

"She served me pizza last weekend."

"So this was before our little race?"

"She gave me the idea," he answers, his smile widening.

"So we raced because some mystery girl told you to?"

"No, we raced because I liked the idea. It sounded fun."

"She told you to," I say.

"She simply said that if she lived in an apartment complex, she would."

"She told you to."

"That's not what I said."

"But it's what you meant."

"Ladies," Sam interrupts, silencing the both of us. "Are you done? I can't eat without thinking you're gonna get spit all over the table."

Our food arrives. Greg and I both remember we're hungry.

"So she's a waitress," I say through a mouthful of pizza. Tasty.

"Yep."

"Where at?" I ask.

"It's a local place."

And something magical happens.

"Hi Greg," says a voice I don't know.

A girl that is tall, with dark red hair almost to

blackness and tanned skin is standing next to our table.

"Hayley, good to see you," says Greg, suddenly beaming again.

"When you came in the first time, I didn't think you meant every day," she says, almost giggling.

I can almost feel Sam's eyebrows raise, mimicking my own incredulity. Greg blushes.

"Number One," I start, raising a finger to signify the number. "No wonder you went on about this place for an hour when we were trying to decide where to go. And Two, every night? Really? You fruit-cup."

"Well it is very good pizza, and Greg speaks highly of you," says Sam.

Clearly a lie, but I let it slide while she's standing right here.

Hayley asks us if we need anything and moves on to the next table.

"So provide me and dear Derek here"—my heart skips a beat—"with actual information concerning our new friend Hayley."

Greg shifts in his seat, and swallows his mouthful of delicious pizza.

"Well, she's currently a student at Voyage University-"

"Voyage University? Is that a *Star Trek* thing?" I ask.

"If you don't want to know, then I won't tell," Greg responds, not smiling.

"Oh, I want to know. I want to know that she's not going to a fictional Space Academy located either in her own head, or in an on-line forum. That'd be good."

"Voyage University is a school for photography. I've been there," Greg says.

"You've been there?" asks Sam, intrigued.

"I graduated from there," he says, annoyed.

Mind blown. Blue screen of death. Restart your computer now.

"I didn't know that," I say, slightly confused. Slightly.

"You didn't ask." Greg lets the silence sink in.

"It's something pretty big to leave out of your life story, which you did voluntarily tell me."

"Did I?"

"Yes."

"Possibly, but you must remember that growing up in a wealthy family, my collegiate degree isn't exactly rare."

"College is still a pretty big chunk of your life though."

"I agree with that," he says. "Hayley and I connected through our mutual experience of college, just like you and Sam through your mutual experience at a funeral."

Awkward Silence. Awkward Coughing and Clearing of Throats. Avert Your Eyes.

"Say what?" Sam says.

"No we didn't," I say. Sam looks at me oddly. I'm uncertain, but I think she's agitated.

"We didn't meet at a funeral," she says. "And why is that even relevant?"

"Well Derek told me you had. And because you're dating."

I hadn't told Greg that we were dating. I hadn't told anyone.

"We're dating?" I say, failing at hiding my nervousness.

"We're not dating," Sam says.

"You two are totally together. Just look at you."

They're both ignoring me. It's as if I could dissolve and they would be oblivious.

Sam looks horrified at this point.

"Derek, please chime in," Greg says, inviting my thoughts out into the open–waving them down with a red flag. This can only go poorly.

"Well, uh," I stumble. "Sam, you never gave me an answer the other day. I've been dreaming about it."

"Dumb idea," Greg mutters.

"Shut up Greg." I'm still looking at Samantha. "Look, I know girls hate it when guys don't give them immediate answers about anything, but guys hate it too. We're aren't robots Sam."

"Robot or not, do you really think this is the place to talk about this?" Sam asks, looking me straight in the eye. "A pizzeria?"

"Not really, but since it's been said–"

"Nothing's been said. I'm gonna go home." Sam gets up and walks away.

"Sam," I say.

"Hey," Greg says, lightly hitting my arm. "Let her cool down for a bit."

But I'm mad at Greg.

"You... I don't have words for you. Shut up and eat your pizza." But I can't eat my own pizza. I get two bites in and give up, and I leave. The walk back to my apartment is short but feels long, and when I sit down on the couch I'm exhausted, but someone knocks on the door and I'm forced to get up to answer.

"Derek?" she says through the door.

Open your eyes, and answer the door. Face her.

I say "Hi."

She says "Hi."

She says that she knows I'm not a robot. But then

she pauses.

"You're the most human person I've ever met, and what's fascinating to me, is that you know it. You're the sweetest guy I've ever met, and it's adorable."

She pauses again, taking a deep breath.

"You talk like no one else I've ever met, and it took a lot of guts to say anything to me at all."

We're still standing in the doorway of my apartment. She doesn't want to come in and I don't want her to go.

"I'm not gonna lie," I say, not quite meeting her eyes. "I've wanted to say this for a while."

And I pause.

"I really really like you."

She smiles. "I like you too."

"Good," I say.

"And I'd love to go on a date with you. And then more dates after that," says Sam.

"I'd love to take you."

"It's a date."

"I told you," says a voice. We look out into the hallway, and Greg's standing there. "It was only a matter of time." And he walks past us and goes into his room.

"Oh shut *up!*" I say.

"Only a matter of time!" he calls, and his door closes.

And there's silence. I don't mind having her to myself for a bit before I have to say goodnight. If I wasn't in love with Samantha before tonight, I am now. I swear with every passing moment, with every breath, I'm falling more in love with this girl, who for some reason doesn't mind my oddball demeanor. My hand slips on the door frame and our fingers touch, but as I move my hand back, Sam places her hand on mine, and laces our fingers together. She's adorable. And perfect. And amazing. After a moment of silence, she steps away.

"Leaving so soon?" I ask.

"I should get some sleep."

"Fine, be that way." I smile. So does she. It's the worlds smallest Festival of Smiles.

"I'll be back tomorrow, okay?" she says.

I nod, still smiling, and I lean against the door frame.

"Maybe we'll go on an adventure," I say.

"I'd like that very much."

"Good night."

"Good night."

She takes my hand, squeezes it, and once she lets go, I close the door. I walk to my bedroom, and I climb into bed, too lazy to undress. I'm ready for sleep.

CHAPTER TWELVE

The viewing has ten minutes to go, and the funeral in half an hour. I may have to speed. I'm most likely going to miss the viewing, and probably most of the service. Despite my first month of dating Sam being fantastic, and that I hadn't been to a funeral in months, I did some quick research, found a funeral, and here I am. Unfortunately, I have had zero time to research anything more than a time or a location, so I'm going in blind. I'm going to have to do my best to stay under the radar, but as always, there are no guarantees.

As I pull up to the funeral home, I'm just in time to join in the final spot of the procession. I put on my flashers and follow closely. The procession only proceeds a few blocks before pulling into the oh-so-familiar cemetery. I know this place like the back of my hand. The long line of cars finally stops, and I can already see the pallbearers carrying the casket toward the grave and setting it down. Waiting for the people to gather around as a collective. As I leave the path to walk alone towards the grave, I notice a girl with red hair. Very dark red, almost black. She's facing away from me, and, for some reason, I make my way over and stop when I'm just a few yards in front of her. I'm still a good distance away from the grave, so I won't attract attention, and no one will wonder why I'm here. Something touches my elbow. I turn, and who should it be, but Hayley, with the dark red hair.

"Hi," she says. There are tears in her eyes.

The rest of the people gathered are still silent, waiting for the Priest to begin his graveside service at the final resting place of Mr. Whomever.

"Hi," I almost whisper, and step backward so that I'm standing next to her. Since I've only known her for a week, and have only spoken to her once, and was rude to her on that occasion, I immediately feel uncomfortable. I also notice that I'm the only one standing next to her.

"I'm very sorry for your loss," I decide to say. "How did you know him?"

And her answer floors me, scares me, astonishes me, and, oddly enough, impresses me.

She leans in, and whispers "Thank you, but I have no idea who he is."

This time when I look at her, the tears are gone and the faint shadow of a smile is on her face. Hayley seems to revel in my speechless

"To me," she continues, "he's Arthur Ingram. He hated his name, loved to go mountain biking, even until his dying day at 56, when it wound up being the cause of his demise."

"What are you—"

"Don't worry," she cuts me off, still whispering. "I can tell a Grave Stalker when I see one. I knew you were one the moment I saw you at the restaurant."

"Excuse me?"

"Grave Stalker," she says, with slightly more authority. "One who visits the graves of the dearly departed in order to enhance the lives of the deceased."

"How do you... what?" I'm shocked.

"But I wouldn't tell anyone that," she says, slyly flashing a smile. "They used to call us Reapers."

"Us?"

"I haven't met many since I started. Welcome to the club."

"Why is this a thing?"

"I don't know, why is it?" she asks.

"You tell me."

"And you tell me why you're at the grave of a dead

man that no one here knows." Her voice gets louder as she speaks.

I look away from the casket. Everyone else is staring at the two of us. Someone coughs.

"Okay," I say, backing away from everyone. "What is this? You said there weren't many."

"There aren't."

"Wait what?" I trip over a headstone. I get up and fix my suit.

"Now they think we're crazy. Time to go, Derek," and with that we turn around to walk to the cars. Slowly at first, our pace quickening until we're almost running. I reach my car and she gets in with me.

"Drive!" she practically yells in my ear. I pull a crude U-turn out of the cemetery and drive down the road, all the way back to my apartment. But I don't stop there. I keep driving. I pull over in front of a small coffee shop.

"Okay," I start, turning to look at her. "What is going on?"

"Hayley Fletcher," Hayley Fletcher says, putting out her hand.

"Derek Wilson. Nice to meet you." We shake hands.

"A pleasure, I'm sure," she says.

"So, back to my first question. What is going on, and how did you know why I was at the funeral?"

"I have a thing for faces. When you stood next to me I recognized you."

"So?" I say. I'm getting an odd feeling.

"So, you had a certain sadness on your face."

"It's a funeral," I say.

"It was a different kind of sadness. A lonely, empty sadness that didn't have anything to do with the people there."

"I think I'm missing the point. Why were *you*

there?"

"I was happy as a kid. Happy as a clam. Then I became a teenager. Things change. You grow up, and it seems that people start to hate you. You start to hate them in return. You feel like the world is mocking you. You're willing to try just about anything, and by the time you're out of college, you've done a lot. A lot of bad things. Drugs. Alcohol. But they didn't work. And one day, you see the obituaries in the newspaper, and you think, why not just go to a funeral? See people who have a reason to be sad. So you do. And it's different. You see people whose tears are real tears."

I can't tell if she's getting worked up because she loves this, or because I'm the first person she's been able to tell, but the tears in her eyes seem real this time.

"These people" she continues, "are truly sad, and then there's you, Derek. Wallowing in your own sorrow. I can see the same look in your eyes that I see in mine."

I let what she said sink in. "Fair enough," I say, my voice hoarse. This girl understands a part of me that no one else has seen. "Well, Greg wasn't happy. But he met you, and his goofy smile won't go away. So now you have a reason to not be sad. And yet, here you are."

"And so are you," she says.

"It felt necessary." I'm not sure I believe me.

"Maybe one could call what we do an obsession," she says.

"Almost certainly," I say, not quite meeting her gaze. She doesn't say anything. "So is it?" I ask, now looking directly at her.

"I don't know," Hayley says. "But we're not so different."

"Is that so?" I put the key in the ignition, and we drive away.

Leaning back on my apartment door so it shuts

behind me, I look up. Greg is sitting on the couch watching a movie.

"Your girlfriend crashed a funeral," I say.

"What?" Greg asks, distracted, not looking away from the TV.

"Nothing."

CHAPTER THIRTEEN

I'm not going to lie, I'm surprised. This week isn't going at all as I imagined. Other than the obvious reason of that Sam and I are a thing now. An official thing. Can I say that? Officially official. Wait. Are we? Officially uncertain. Officially confused. Greg's officially here.

"Hey, sweetheart," Greg says. He's leaning against the doorway in my bedroom. The door is wide open. I don't remember closing it, so it's probably my fault.

"Hullo," I'm still too tired to think straight. At least out loud.

"Can you believe it? Dude, so, we're both taken men."

"It's been how long?" I mumble. "I bet you still don't know much about her." I prop myself up on the bed to look at Greg, and he smiles this goofy smile at me, and he stumbles forward, turning at the right moment so that when he falls, he lands in a sitting position on the bed.

"She likes pizza."

"What amazing depth."

"She loves Daft Punk, and Jane Austen books–"

"Yes, I'd forgotten all the times you've told me about your passion for Daft Punk and tales of Austen," I slide in between his sentences.

"Don't interrupt me"

"Won't happen again."

"She enjoys going to music stores to buy CD's she's never heard of, and she dislikes the high prices of vinyl."

"How does she feel about film?" I wonder.

"Uh, sometimes it pays to let someone finish talking."

"Not usually."

"Quite right. Anyway, Hayley loves going to the *theatre*," Greg says, standing up, and almost dancing his way around the room. He practically glides on my floor and exits.

"We're going to see The Great Gatsby next week!" he calls from the next room.

"Don't you hate Fitzgerald?"

"Regardless of my displeasure for dear F. Scott," Greg reappears in the doorway of my bedroom, by holding onto the inside of the frame and swinging outward. "I am perfectly willing to put up with him for one night so I can enjoy being in the company of the wonderfully intoxicating Hayley Fletcher."

"That's cute," I muse. It's hard to keep from laughing at him.

"So," Greg says, standing up and walking to the couch. He sits, smirking. "How about you?"

PART TWO

one year later

CHAPTER FOURTEEN

Greg tells me to sit down. He places me at the head of my table, himself on my left and Hayley on my right. Greg is the one who called this meeting. Definitely not me. As much as I trust them, I wouldn't trust them with this.

"Tell her what you told me," Greg says.

"This better be good, I'm missing my show for this," says Hayley.

"Your 'show' is HGTV. It'll be exactly the same when you get back," Greg says. He looks at me, and nods his head hurriedly. Hayley's giving me a death stare.

"Spit it out, Sparky," she says.

"Okay... I'm gonna propose."

Greg just stares at me, stone faced, and Hayley's face is scrunched up. She's either confused or disgusted.

"You know, we've been dating a year. How surprised can you be?" I say, gesturing to Hayley.

"No no no," Hayley hurriedly says, "I'm definitely happy for you, I'm just surprised you made it this long!"

"*We*," Greg says, pointing enthusiastically at Hayley and himself, "think you're going to need some help." He looks at Hayley, who glares back at him. "A lot of help," he corrects himself.

"You're the worst," I say.

"Tell me you have a plan," Hayley says.

"It would be better if you didn't, though," says Greg.

"I have a plan."

"It's probably awful, but let's hear it," says Hayley.

"First, we're going to go out to dinner–" I start, but

Hayley interrupts.

"Terribly cliché. What next?"

"The. Worst." I say. "After dinner we'd go for a walk in the park. Just something nice." I shrug.

"Where in the park?" Hayley asks.

"Down the path near the bottom of the hill. Just before the halfway marker," I say. "Then we'll stop and at the right moment you can take a picture on your phone. If you want."

"Someone better be taking pictures," Greg says. "I think we'd all love to remember this for years." He looks up at the wall behind Hayley, like it's a TV. "Look! There's the moment she rejected him! Aww now he's crying. Ahh, memories!" His grin turns into a wide, goofy smile. Hayley waves him away and turns back to me.

"You've got a ring, right?"

"Of course," I say, reaching into my pocket and pulling out a small box. She takes it from me and pops it open. Her jaw slacks ever so slightly.

"We need to do this right." She stops, and looks at Greg. "Greg, I need you."

He looks bemused. "Okay..."

"Go away," she says. "Go to the park, go shopping. Go. And take Sam with you. We need to keep her out of the way." She pauses. "Actually, go grocery shopping. Don't you have a list?"

He gets up, begrudgingly, but he goes. Grabbing his coat and walking out the door, mumbling about responsibilities. I look at Hayley, expectant, but she's watching the door. After a few seconds of listening, she scoots her chair back and motions for me to follow.

She leads me out the door and up the stairs all the way to the roof, where I stop and she looks around, inspecting.

She walks around the roof twice before stopping by

the edge in front of me, looking over the side, and then off into the distance, and she turns to look at me, smiling.

"Here," she says.

"Here what?"

"Propose here."

"Why would I do that?" I ask.

"Because the park is a terrible idea, trust me."

"I do trust you, but I would like to have a reason," I say.

"Come on, Derek. This is a thousand times better than a cheesy walk in the park in front of everybody. I know she wouldn't want a super public proposal, and I know *you* definitely don't want that." She looks around again. "This is perfect."

"So what do I do?" I ask.

"Picture this," she says.

**

It's particularly warm for April. Greg and Sam have been shopping for an hour, and Hayley and I are sitting on a bench in the park, waiting for them to come back. Hayley looks at the path ahead of us and says "At any moment, we're gone. Poof, that's it. Say goodbye and forget all your hopes."

"You're feeling chipper today," I say.

She ignores my comment and turns to look at me. "What do you think?" she asks.

"I think there are other things to worry about."

"Like what?"

"Like if Greg is going to remember that I'm out of

mayonnaise," I say, trying my best to sound serious.

"I hope he forgets," she says.

"You're meaner than I thought you would be," I say.

"Oh boo hoo," she says. "People aren't daisies and sunshine twenty-four seven."

"I can dream."

"And you do," she says, looking at me. "Life is disappointing. We forget what we hoped we'd always remember, our lifelong goals fade away, and our roommates forget to buy more mayonnaise. It's the way the world works."

Hayley has done surprisingly little to help me with this venture. Her main purpose seems to be to shoot down my ideas when I offer them. As we sit on the bench she points out various trees and what she thinks their names are. I don't know their names either but I play along.

"'Carcerous,'" she says, pointing to another one.

"Sounds right," I say, not even looking where she's pointing.

"Yeah, I think so too." Her phone buzzes. "They're on their way back. Let's go."

While I'm trying not to trip over the uneven bricks in the walkway, Hayley has no trouble maneuvering her way around, moving gracefully along the path.

"You know," she says. "You and I have a connection."

"Sure," I say, only half paying attention.

"We know more about each other than the others do."

"I suppose so."

"We do," she says, and I notice she's stopped walking. She's staring at me now. "We have a mutual respect for the dead."

"I'm not sure I'd call it that," I say.

"I would," she says. "We share that bond, and because of that, I have to say something."

"What?"

"I don't know how this is going to end. I don't know where I'm going to end up in a year, or even in a month. No matter what, regardless of what happens to myself and Greg, I'll be around when you need me. Okay? I promise."

"Thanks," I say, unsure of how to take this sudden offer. "I'll do the same for you," I assure her.

"Thanks for letting me be involved with this, as well." She's nodding her head. "I think we've been pretty great friends," she says. "And without great friends, we'd all be in a psych ward. Come on, let's hurry up and get back."

**

Greg, Hayley, and I spent the afternoon setting the stage. We pooled together all our candles and placed them on a corner of the parapet where we set a table and two lawn chairs, after all, we only had a day. I'm waiting on the roof dressed like a waiter for Hayley to lead Samantha up, and then I can surprise her. I've been waiting for a while so instead of waiting on my mark, I'm wandering around the roof, taking in the different views of the city. I'm standing on the opposite side of the entrance, so when the door opens and I hear Sam say my name, I have to walk around the side.

She's wearing a light blue dress that falls just past her knees, and she looks amazing. Hayley and I put out a table with two chairs with champagne glasses, and there are

"Hi," I say.

"Hey there," she says back. She walks over and we hug. She's crazy comfortable. She lets go, and looks around, noticing the lawn chairs that are sitting a few feet from the edge. "What's going on?"

"I've really only been thinking about one thing lately," I say.

"What one thing?"

"I'm just trying to figure things out, and I thought I'd like to spend more time with you."

"That's so sweet," she says, a wide smile appearing on her face.

"I've realized that I'd like to spend as much time with you as possible."

I reach into my pocket and pull out the little box, and I kneel down as I open it up and show it to her. She puts her hand over her mouth to hide her even wider smile, and out of the corner of my eye I can see Hayley and Greg standing in the doorway of the stairwell taking pictures with their phones.

"Samantha, would you do me the honor of becoming my wife?"

The tears are starting to fall down her face but she nods her yes over and over and after I slip the ring onto her finger, I stand up and we hug tighter than ever.

CHAPTER FIFTEEN

As October rolls into town, the loss of September and of Summer strike me hard. Those are my favorite months, now a thing of the past as I trudge through the brown leaves falling around me. The winding paths take me on indirect routes that would confuse anyone who had no idea what they're looking for. But I know what I seek. I see a lot of names; names that I don't know.

A warm breeze blows through my leather jacket. I miss the Summer. I miss days so hot that the only sensible thing to do was to crank up the air conditioning and stay in to watch movies with Greg. Sam and Hayley visit often. Dinners, movies, shows. We do it all.

I've been missing someone. Now I'm standing at his grave. Dad. We last "spoke" when you appeared in my dream so many months ago. But now when I need to talk to you the most, you don't appear.

I stand motionless, staring at the name on the stone. Wilson. I feel honored to have that name. I lay flowers on the grave. Cemeteries. I'm growing weary of this place. Necessary though it may be.

"Hi Dad." Sometimes formalities are still needed. Even if the conversation is entirely one-sided.

"It's been a while. I miss you. A lot. I, uh, I just wanted to drop by and say Hello. It 's been a long time since you died. You didn't pass away. You didn't slip away. You died. No sense in putting a veil over it. God has you now. I can't get you back. I'd do anything to talk to you face to face. I need your advice again. No funny questions, or riddles, or obvious questions with obvious answers that I still don't know how to answer. I have some serious problems."

I pause. A bird chirps. A woman laughs. I look over at her. She's walking with a man and holding hands.

"I remember, one thing you told me when I was sixteen: 'When everything seems to be going wrong, talk to Him. When everything's perfect, talk to Him. You'll need it. Things have a tendency to work out eventually when you do.'"

I pause. And something seems to click. Suddenly I'm walking around feverishly, perplexed, stressed.

"And I'm supposed to talk to You?" I yell to the sky. "You took him away from me, and I'm still supposed to trust You? This is You in control? Do You even know what's going on down here?" My words are swept away by the wind, with no reply. "Greg, who's been more like a brother to me than my actual brother, is out of the apartment and sleeping on Hayley's couch. I don't hear anything from him. No calls, no anything. I've left message after message, and still nothing. I can only apologize so many times. What am I supposed to do? Just sit tight and hold on?"

I turn away and walk two graves over. I turn back.

"I miss him. I do. He was my first friend, and now he's gone. Hayley won't tell me what's happening. Is there something you're waiting on me to do, or what?"

Aggravated, feeling worse than I did when I got here, I trudge back down the winding paths. Stupid winding paths. Who lays out a cemetery with no structure? No grid. Just a path here and there. Different sections: A. B. C. Lost and found. Broken and restored.

Forsaken and Forgiven.

I leave and after five minutes of walking I stop. Leaning against a wall, then sliding to the ground. Head in my hands, I can hear the sounds around me. People talking, random laughter. I look up and take in my surroundings. Across the street is a café. Chairs and tables are set up outside. I decide to get up and go home, when someone close by yells at me, and I hear hurried footsteps. I turn to look, but suddenly it's very hot, something hits me and I'm thrown into the air, and then nothing.

CHAPTER SIXTEEN

I hear only screaming. Deafening inside my brain, the noise echoes through my throat so my voice is screaming in unison with my mind. Intense pain rips through my body, reaching all my limbs, and I receive a massive jolt causing me to sit up, still screaming, eyes wide open, and my arm reaching out. Blackness.

**

In and out. The darkness. The pain. Red. Black. Switching between opaqueness and transparency. Fog and clarity. More pain. A woman's face is clear only for a fraction of a second, before it distorts and flows in my vision, seeping away, leaving my sight. Loss of consciousness. Becoming more frail by the second. The pain is blinding; the only gift it brings is darkness, but what a phony blessing it is.

**

Standing still and alone in the middle of the street. One foot on each yellow line. A car is visible, approaching me quickly. The car is speeding, faster and faster with every second, and I remain motionless, my eyes locked on the vehicle, daring it to come closer. Daring it to hit me. The car revs, I can hear it from where I stand, and it swerves until it's over the center lines in the road, directly in my way. Except now I'm in its way. It's a hundred feet away. Faster. Fifty feet. Fifteen feet. I flinch right before–

I open my eyes and I'm staring at the ceiling. My view widens, and I see machines. My ears pick up a steady beeping. I'm in a hospital room. A hospital bed, to be more accurate. There's no one by my side, but there is a large pile of flowers and overflowing baskets wrapped in plastic on a table in the corner. I attempt to sit up, and a sharp pain shoots from my left arm, causing me to yelp in pain, and it refuses to move. My left arm is heavily bandaged and in a sling. I also notice a large bandage on my chest, under my gown. It's right above my right pectoral. I poke it. Yep. Definitely hurts. The beeping speeds up for a few seconds.

"I can't help falling in love with you," says a voice to my left, echoing slightly. Almost distant.

"What?" I say, turning to look, but the searing pain returns, threatening to tear my chest apart. My eyes water, and my hand clenches, holding my bedsheets captive in my fist. The beeping emanating from the machine escalates until it's almost a steady line, barely pausing in between noises.

The pain is blinding once again, and blurred shapes of varying colors rush around me and I feel hands on me, holding me down, but I don't care. At this point I would rather die than endure the constant stabbing pain.

And as the darkness wraps me in its welcoming arms once more, I succumb and embrace the Dark.

It's nice to see you.

"You too," a voice whispers in my ear. She hugs me. "You finally came," she speaks again.

"I don't know you," I'm saying.

A shock hits me, and I stumble backwards.

"They're trying to bring you back."

"Do I have to go back?" I groan. I'm not feeling so

well.

"No," she says. She's very pretty. Even with half of her face charred, peeling and deformed, the lesser scars extending over the rest of her face. It's a shame she's here. "I'd prefer it if you stayed. We all would."

"All?"

"All of us. Here." And a crowd appears behind her. Some of them bloodied, and some just dirty. All of them look depressed at the thought of me leaving, as though they'd known me their entire lives. One of them, a man, steps forward. He shakes my hand.

"I'm waiting for my wife to join me. I know I'm supposed to be here, and she'll be here one day too. You're not as far gone as I was. It's still your choice."

I look closely at the man. He's transparent. I can see the crowd behind him. *Through* him.

"Where am I?" I ask.

Another jolt hits me, shaking me so I have to regain my balance. I hold out my arms to steady myself. Both arms. I can use my left arm here.

"You mean," she says, "you don't know?"

"Know what?" I ask, frustrated.

"You really don't know?"

"No, I don't!" I yell at them. Everyone backs away except for her. She remains motionless, but she looks concerned.

"The attack. You were there. You saw."

And slowly, I do see. The loud bang. Fire. Glass shattering. People thrown into the air. More people hitting the ground. I hit the ground. I touch my left arm. My left hand is missing it's pinkie, and I can see my leg as well. I see that my left pants leg is missing most of the material, and my leg is incomplete, and I collapse, trying to remember everything that happened.

"So who am I?" I ask, suddenly realizing that I don't

know who I am.

"I was hoping you would tell me, sweetie," she says, walking slowly towards me, and kneeling on the ground in front of me.

Eye level. Vertical. Oncoming traffic. Parallel. Gravity. Flight.

I notice one thing. There's some kind of fluid on the ground beneath me. I stare at it, and despite the darkness I can see my own reflection. There's blood trickling down the side of my face, disappearing and reappearing again.

"They're trying to fix you up," she says, her left hand reaching out and touching my face.

"Where am I?" I ask again. Overwhelming fear and underwhelming knowledge.

"You're here because of me," she says, ignoring my question.

"What? Why?"

"Because I killed you," she says, her voice very small.

Oh. *Oh.*

"So I'm dead?" I say, angry and confused.

"Technically yes."

"And everyone else?"

"They actually *are* dead."

I stand up, towering above her.

"What did you do?" I'm yelling at her.

"I couldn't stop it," she says quietly, tears forming in her eyes.

"Stop *what*?" I yell.

"The bomb!" she screams back, tears streaming from her face.

There's silence except for her sobs. I'm standing over her, raging inside my own mind.

"So where exactly are we?" I ask, trying to be as calm as possible, gritting my teeth.

"Inside your head."

"What?"

"You're in a coma!" she says, still sobbing.

You're in a coma-... Processing... processing... Please login... Password incorrect... Password incorrect... Password accepted... Enter command... Command "Identity"... No such command...

"I wish you would wake up...." says a disembodied voice, echoing into the blackness.

I look at the girl in front of me, and images flash before me. I'm walking down the street outside the cemetery, and I see her running towards me, clearly in a hurry.

"I saw you," I say. "What happened?"

"It's complicated," she says. "I tried to stop it, and I tried warning people, but I failed."

A faint, steady beeping is heard. Peculiar.

"What's your name?" I ask.

"Olivia," she says after a moment.

The beeping is getting slower, more spaced out.

"Olivia. You blew me up. By accident."

I look at her, and I see her. Really see her. I see the sadness in her eyes. I see her burnt and scarred face, beautified by the fresh tear tracks.

"At least you tried," I say.

She smiles at me, and just as she does, the beeping comes to a crescendo and falls into one steady note, my knees hit the ground, I'm gasping for breath.

"I'll miss you," Olivia says, and she fades into the darkness as she walks away.

I feel another jolt, knocking me flat to the ground this time. Bright lights are flashing all around me. I feel sick. I see faces warping in and out, some coming and some going. I recognize none of them.

CHAPTER SEVENTEEN

I sit up, gasping, pulling air back into my grateful lungs, and a woman runs up to me, pushing the doctors aside, her hands on me, hugging me, trying to push me back onto the bed. But I can't see her on my left. I can't see anything to my left. I automatically put my hands up to my eyes, panicking.

"Derek!" she's crying. Hugging me again.

"My eye," I say. "I can't see!"

I look at the faces around me, waiting for them to help.

"Why can't I see?!" I yell. The doctors have disappeared. There are two women and a man standing around my bed, and another man sitting in the chair near the back of the room. I look at them with only my right eye. They look scared but no one moves.

"What's wrong with my eyes??"

A doctor comes back in and puts his hands up, a light in one.

"We're going to take a look, okay?" I freeze, and look at him from the right. He shines the light in my face and moves it from one eye to the other. I can see the light in my left eye as if it were closed and the light was shining through my eyelid.

"We were worried this might happen," the doctor says, "but I think the blindness is temporary. Your vision should return to you shortly. Other than that, how are you feeling?"

"We're so glad you're back, sweetheart," the

younger woman says.

"Good to know you're still hanging on, Bud." says the man to my left, and he sighs.

My left arm and my chest are still covered in wrapping. Not much pain though. I notice my leg this time, blood has stained the wrapping. It's odd and a little creepy to look at, so I look back at the small crowd.

"Derek?" the woman asks. "What's wrong?"

"Who are you?" I ask.

"It's me," she says, a tear forming in her eye. "Sam. Samantha. You know me, Derek."

I shake my head, and I feel sorry for the woman as her knees seem to give out a little beneath her.

The other woman, much older than the first, comes forward and stands on the left side of my bed.

"I'm your Mother, Derek. Do you remember me?" She's staring at me.

"You don't remember any of us?" the man in the back says, also looking concerned.

The woman who says she's my mother says "You were at our house for dinner last month."

The man on the other side of the bed says "You're my brother." They take turns feeding me lines, trying to spark some recognition.

She says "Your Father and I took you and your brother to Maine every year..."

"Remember Dad? Mom?" he gestures to the woman, who looks as if she's about to have a heart attack, and I can do nothing but sit here and watch these people fall apart before my eyes.

Looking warily at me, the other man rises from the

chair, his blond hair falling in front of his face. "It's me, Greg."

And they all start speaking at once.

"I'm your fiancée."

"I'm your Mommy."

"We hated each other."

"I'm your best friend."

"How could you not remember me?"

"We live in the same building."

I look back at Greg. He falls silent. Staring.

I can't remember. My head hurts, my brain is screaming and I'm just trying to remember anything.

Greg's standing beside the bed, unable to look away. I can see the old woman now in the hallway and watch her collapse into a chair.

I feel so sorry for them. I *am* so sorry.

The two doctors move Greg aside, and converge on me, one fumbling with a needle and a tiny bottle, the other standing over me, flashing a light in my eyes and peppering me with questions.

"What is your name?"

"I don't know."

"Where are you from?"

"I don't know."

"What year is it?"

"I don't know."

"How old are you?"

"I don't know."

"And you don't know who these people are?"

"No."

I don't remember anything. In a single act, a single moment, every memory, relationship, conversation and emotion I've ever had is gone. In an instant I've lost everything.

But then there's this woman, gripping my hand as if she'll die without it.

**

Three weeks in that hospital. They let me out today. They tell me my name is Derek Wilson. Twenty-nine years old. My Father is dead, survived by his wife. I have one sibling, a brother. I think his name is Marshall. I have a best friend named Greg, and I have a fiancée named Samantha.

That's what I know. That's what they tell me. Everything else is forgotten. Everything else doesn't exist.

I'm in this apartment that they say is mine. Upon entering one of the bedrooms I see a large stack of money in the corner that, when I counted it, amounts to about eight-hundred-and-fifty-thousand dollars. A lot. Hmm.

The apartment is nice. Apparently I'm very clean and organized. Hundreds of books line the shelves, mixed with an ocean of blue with specks of black for all the Blu-Rays and DVDs. These are all mine. The furniture is without dust, or even a hint of frequent use. It's as if it's a model, waiting to be wrapped in plastic and stored for the rest of eternity. Hmm.

Someone knocks on the door and I do my best to walk on my good leg and I answer the door. It's Samantha. She inches away as I open the door, almost frightened. Her eyes are red from either lack of sleep or crying.

"Yeah?" I say. I just want her to leave.

"Hi," she says.

"Hi." My leg is starting to hurt so I put my hand on the door frame.

She looks at me. It's probably hard for her to see me like this.

I step aside to let her by. Samantha walks around the room, and though I'm not looking at her, I can tell she's looking at me.

"You still don't remember me, do you?"

I shake my head. "No."

"How have you been sleeping?" she asks, nervously glancing at me.

"I do okay," I say.

"Do you like it here?" she asks.

I turn and walk into the room on the left side, Samantha following me. This is the bedroom. The bed itself is large, and altogether too big for one person. I walk over to the wardrobe and open it. Numerous drawers and doors open up to reveal hundreds of different clothing combinations, organized by occasion, that I could never exhaust, even if I never wore another article twice. I go into the bathroom, but after a quick glance I walk back out.

"All of this is mine." I say, sitting down on the couch.

"Yeah."

"It's a bit much."

Sam stands in the doorway to the other bedroom, looks in, and turns back to me. "Looks like Greg left you a lot," she says. "You might want to put all that in the bank."

"Why did he leave me that much?" I ask.

"He probably wants you to not have to worry about anything for a while," she shrugs.

"More than already, you mean?"

She forces a small laugh, and her face returns to normal. "Have you read any of your scripts?"

"Not a word."

"Do you know where they are?" she asks.

"I think I saw a box of papers but I didn't bother with it."

"You're not curious?"

"Not really," I say. "Why? Do you want them?"

"No, no!" she says, putting up her hands to face me. "They're yours."

"It's no trouble at all," I say, standing up.

I walk to my office and begin searching, Samantha protesting from the other room. I sift through boxes and drawers and folders that contain papers, bank documents, past resumes and finally find a box that is heavy with set after set of bound papers. I hastily pick through them to make sure they are indeed written by Derek Wilson before closing the box again. I carry the box back to the kitchen, and set it on the counter.

"Here you go, all yours," I say forcing a smile.

"No, I don't want— you should keep it," she's saying, pushing the box towards me.

"I don't think I'll be needing it anymore," I say,

putting my hand on the box to stop it from moving. "Just take them," I say, and, with sadness, she takes the box. She walks away, but stops at the door and turns around.

"Derek..." she starts, again unable to look me in the face. "I still love you. Remember that, please." She looks at me for a long time, and she leaves.

And for the first time in recent weeks, I'm alone, and there is silence.

CHAPTER EIGHTEEN

Now a week later, I've been reading up on memory loss, and what I've discovered is that it's almost a certainty I'll never remember anything before a month ago. No one has even told me what happened. All I know is the identity of my immediate circle: Greg, Samantha, my mother, and my brother. I'm in the middle of putting on this shirt, which has two zippers (why, I have no idea) when I glance around and notice a woman I don't know in my living room. She has red hair so dark that at first glance it seems black, and her tanned skin is striking in the brightness of my apartment. Maybe it's just my eyes, still imperfect.

"Hi, Derek," she says, half-smiling.

"Hi," I say, frozen. "Who, ah—?"

"Who am I? Hayley. I'm Greg's girlfriend," she says, and sits down on the couch.

"Ah, right," I respond. "I've heard a lot about you."

"Good things, I hope."

"Of course." I say. "And how did you get in?"

"I have a key. I'm sorry it took so long for me to come by. I had to figure out how I was going to approach you."

"Approach me?" I say.

"The situation between you and I required a lot of thought," she says.

"What situation?" I ask. "Things are difficult for me right now, so, if you have something important to say, you can start now."

"I know it's difficult. How's the eye?" she asks.

"You're a little fuzzy, but I'm fine. So what are you here for?"

"I have something important to show you," she says.

"Okay."

"It's not here," she says, and gestures to the door.

"And you expect me to get into a car with you?"

"Yes," she says.

"Are you gonna tell me what this is about, at least?" I ask.

"It's hard to explain."

"Try."

"It'll be more easier to show you. Just come with me."

"Where?" I ask.

"Someplace very essential to who you are."

Twenty minutes later she pulls over and we're outside a funeral home. She hands me an obituary.

"'Lewis Jefferson, thirty-five. Worked as an electrician. Died last week on the job'," I say. "Why are we here?" I ask.

"Get out of the car," she says. "We're going in there, and we're doing what we do best."

"Which is what?" I ask.

"Reminisce," she says calmly.

"What?" I say, stepping out of the car. "I didn't know the guy."

"Not this version of Lewis. You knew a different one."

"A different one..." I say, bewildered.

"Yep."

"That makes sense," I mutter.

Hayley walks to the door and opens it.

"In," she says, nodding. I walk in.

I follow her into the Jefferson room, and I'm immediately out of place. I'm under-dressed, and not only do I know none of the people packed into this room, I don't even know who Lewis Jefferson is. I'm not even *supposed* to know who these people are.

Hayley signs the guest book for both of us, walks confidently into the crowd and I follow, tentatively. She stops in front of a memorial wall that someone put up, with pictures tacked to it of Lewis throughout his life, flowers on the floor surrounding the base. I ease alongside her, and follow her gaze at the pictures. I watch her face from the corner of my eye. Hayley's face is so downcast, and full of sadness, it's hard to believe that five minutes ago she was looking at me with an upbeat face.

It's just us, standing before this tribute to our departed friend Lewis. The people around us do not acknowledge our presence. We remain there in silence. Family and friends stand next to us, and we make no attempt to engage them; we wait for them to leave.

One lone soul remains.

"He was a beautiful man," this person says, and I turn to look at her. Tears in her eyes, the woman brings a tissue to her face and wipes them away. I say nothing, and Hayley says nothing.

"He would bring me flowers every Friday night,

and he'd let me pick a movie for us both to watch."

I look around the room, then back at the pictures. A man, his life gone. Only a woman left behind to weep. She asks,

"How did you know him?"

"I didn't," says Hayley. "My friend knew him."

Wait, *what?*

"Um," I start, not liking that I'm on the spot. "He taught me how to... drive," I stammer.

Punch me in the face and kick my leg out from under me.

"Oh, really?"

"Uh, yeah," I say, positive that the uncertainty in my voice will give me away.

"That's wonderful. I hope he did a good job."

"Well, only I would know," I say, attempting a smile.

"How long did it take?" she asks.

"About two weeks."

Gaining confidence now.

"That's amazing." But something's not right. She looks right at me. "Because, Lewis didn't drive. He was terrified of the road."

Oh no.

"So," she continues, her voice sending chills down my spine. "How about you tell me who you really are, and why you're disturbing us."

The room suddenly feels claustrophobic, despite no one being around us.

"We were just leaving," I say, and, as I walk away (hurrying without hurrying) I notice some people turn their heads and start to follow us.

I'm out the door with Hayley in tow and head for the car; I get in but Hayley is taking forever to get to the driver's side. When she's finally in, she starts the car and, before her seatbelt is even buckled, we're racing down the road at almost twice the speed limit.

"What was that?" I yell at her. "What was the point? Why would you do that to me?"

"The point was to get you thinking," she says calmly.

"About what?"

"About who you really are."

"I'm me!"

"Then clearly it didn't work!" she yells back, jerking the wheel to turn down an alley, and she stops the car. "The Derek Wilson that I know would've had some fantastic story about going mountain climbing with Lewis Whatever-His-Name-Was and his wife would've believed it. The Derek Wilson I knew would have been cool and not rushed out. He would have talked his way out of it, because the Derek Wilson I knew wasn't afraid of being in a bad situation. He would have accepted it, adapted to it, and joined right in."

A moment of silence for me.

"Then I'm not who you think I am."

"Apparently not," Hayley says, her voice downtrodden. She reaches down into her purse and pulls out a newspaper clipping. "You should have this," she says, handing it to me. It's Lewis' obituary.

"You collected them. One for every funeral."

I stare at it.

The day is wasted on the dead. My life is being wasted on the living.

Derek Wilson is not a real person. Derek Wilson doesn't exist. Derek Wilson is a figment of everyone else's imagination. He's a fake. He's patient. He has family and friends. I, on the other hand, have ghosts. I have strangers. Every day is a subway ride next to a complete stranger who won't stop talking to me.

My drivers license says Derek Jacob Wilson, and while he's dead, I live in his apartment, listed as *TwentyForty Factory Street.* Every morning I wake up in his bed. I eat from his dishes, dress in his fancy clothes, stare at his bookshelves lined with hundreds of books and movies that I've never read or seen. The sea of blue cases is incredible. People spend money on these things. Actual money. I spend time outside on walks to the park and around town, seeing life for the first time. Meeting people for the first time, familiar or strange. My second life as a human is a test of crash and burn and try again. Resurrection at its poorest.

It's time for a fresh start. I'm feeling very tired of the name Derek Jacob Wilson, and I relieve my mind of that burden.

CHAPTER NINETEEN

The Lewis Jefferson fiasco has influenced some of my behavior, like my new title of Aaron Foley. Lately I've found myself alone a lot in Derek's apartment, which honestly isn't so bad.

I sit down on the couch in the living room and look up at the ceiling. Everything is beige and bland, except the coffee table in front of me, and the TV. I get up from the couch and go to the kitchen and open the fridge. A lot of boxed meals, cartons of eggs, bacon, various condiments, almost all expired, and a glass pan of what appears to be a casserole. Gross. In the drawer I find plenty of small chocolates, so I eat one. The drinks in the door consist of water, expired milk, and orange juice.

Closing the fridge, I move on to the cabinets above the counter. A good amount of dishes for someone who lives alone, I think. Nice dishes, too. Nothing plastic, all glass or porcelain. Satisfied, I close those and open the drawers by the sink. Silverware. And lots of it. I close the drawer and turn around too quickly, tripping on my bad foot and falling to the floor, my vision flashing when my head makes contact, my left eye suddenly letting me see.

"Ow!" I moan. "Ughh." I push myself up and sit, rubbing my head and wincing. It's not perfect, the image slightly blurry and everything is moving, like TV static. "I guess it's something," I mutter. I stand up and walk to my bathroom, still massaging my head. Looking closely at my head in the mirror, I notice the scars on my face. The most noticeable is diagonal from my forehead to just above my cheek, interrupted by my left eye which looks almost gray. I close my right eye and stare at my reflection, and it's nothing but skewed lines and static. I re-open my right eye, look myself up and down once more and turn to leave, but beyond my bedroom I see a woman sitting at the counter.

"Whoa!" I yell, and she jumps. "Get out!"

And she's startled and almost falls out of the chair, and she's yelling too. "Hey, listen, I'm not here to hurt you!"

But I'm not listening, moving towards her and motioning for her to leave. "Get out of my house!"

And she's protesting. "It's not what you think!"

But I'm yelling. "Get out, get out, get out!"

"I'm not really here!"

I stop, and she stops, still about fifteen feet away from each other.

"You're here," I say. "I can see you."

"Yeah, okay, and I get that that's confusing," she says. "But I promise you, I'm not exactly real."

She steps forward cautiously, coming closer.

"I'm dead," she says.

"Right, okay." And then I remember. "You're her," I say. "You're the girl from before."

She tilts her head, and stops. "Before?"

"Before I woke up I was in a coma and I saw a girl. You're her."

"I don't think so," she says.

But now I'm worried. "You really need to leave."

"I don't think that's a good idea," she says, putting up a hand.

"It definitely is," I say. "You have to go." I move

forward as quickly as I can, shooing her through the door and locking it.

"No you don't understand, this is important!" her muffled voice calls from the other side. I move back and grab my phone on the counter, looking at the pile of papers on the counter—the residue from my hospital stay. I find my doctor's number and speedily repeat the numbers on my phone. It rings twice before he answers.

"Hello?" he says.

"Hello, Doctor Laien?" I ask urgently.

"Yes, who's this?" he asks.

"Derek Wilson."

"Oh yes, how are you feeling?"

"Good news and bad," I say. "My left eye started working, but it's a little blurry, and I'm seeing things."

"What kinds of things?"

"People, Doc!" I say, knowing that he'll probably think I'm crazy.

"Who?"

"I don't know," I say.

"Anyone you know or recognize?"

"Maybe, she-"

And suddenly the door opens and the girl is back.

"Oh no you don't, this won't end well for you!" she says.

"Doc!" I yell, terrified as she runs at me and knocks the phone out of my hands, which shatters on the floor.

"Do you have any idea what you've just done?" she demands.

"I talked to my doctor," I offer.

"You basically told him you're crazy."

"I told him about a medical issue," I say.

"And he's going to interpret that as a psychological issue."

"This might be a psychological issue!"

She shoves me and I fall backward onto my butt.

"Did that feel psychological to you?" she asks.

"How can you touch me if you're not real?"

"I'm a ghost," she says.

"Oh really?" I ask. "So I can see you, and I can touch you?"

"Well that's what I think I am."

"Okay," I say. "So *why* can I see you?"

She kneels down next to me. "I'm betting that it has to do with that eye of yours," and she points.

I close my left eye, and she disappears, but I can see the outline of her figure. "*That's* different," I say. "So if you're a ghost, what am I?" I ask. "Am I broken?"

"No, you're not broken," Olivia says, sitting down next to me.

"Then what am I?"

"You're alive," she says.

"That's great, but so is everyone else. So what's wrong with me that I can see you?"

"Why does there have to be something wrong with you? Why isn't there something wrong with everyone else that they can't see me?" she asks. "I'm not really thrilled about seeing you, either. But I don't know what's wrong with you or anyone else, for that matter. To some extent *all* people are crazy. You're all in need of psychiatric help on some level. But it's not going to come."

"That's great news and all, but it's not much comfort coming from *you*, you know? The whole being dead thing isn't reassuring to those of us who aren't."

"I don't know why you can see me. But you can still help me."

"Help you what?" I ask.

"I need to see my body."

Olivia's face starts to change. It becomes scarred, the skin starts to darken and some disappears entirely, revealing rotting flesh beneath, and again I recognize her. In that dark corner somewhere in my brain, an image floats to the front of my mind: Olivia in her newly revealed form, distraught, crying and on the ground, with only an angry version of myself standing over her, and I am yelling.

"Wow," I say.

Olivia smiles, and the scars worsen, deepening in her once beautiful face, now deformed.

"Can't you look in a mirror?" I suggest.

"I don't appear in reflections," she snaps, and I feel stupid.

"Why do you want to do this?" I ask.

"I just think it's something I have to do."

"Alright then," I say, a little creeped out. "Where is your body?"

"Where any corpse would be," she says.

"Right. Cemetery."

"Duh."

"Where?" I ask.

"That's your job," she replies.

"I'm supposed to help you find where you're buried? And how will this help me?"

"In a perfect world?" she asks. "I'll leave you alone."

**

Prowling through a cemetery looking for a grave to exhume at three in the morning, guided by the poor light of a dying flashlight, is not something I ever thought I would do.

"Aaron, are you sure you know where you're going?" Olivia is walking alongside me peering at the headstones as we pass.

"I was until you said something," I say, throwing down the shovel and looking at the papers I had printed out.

"When you said you looked it up I assumed you would know what you're doing."

"Come on, where are you?" I say, scrutinizing the map. "I don't think we're far…"

"It's over here, dummy," says Olivia, two rows away.

"How do you know?"

"I knew the entire time," she says.

"You let me wander around this place for half an hour and you didn't say anything?"

"Basically."

"What's the matter with you?" I ask, annoyed.

"I'm dead."

"Other than that." I say. "You're really messed up, you know that right?"

"I'm not the one seeing a dead girl."

"So my imaginary friend let me dig up a dead girl in an effort to help bury another dead girl... Yeah that makes sense," I say, trudging along a good fifteen feet behind Olivia.

"I'm not imaginary!" she calls over her shoulder.

"Quiet down!" I hiss. "You're gonna—"

"Gonna what? Wake up the dead people?"

"You're really good at making me feel stupid," I mutter under my breath.

"I'm honored to fill the position," she calls over her shoulder.

Olivia stops. And there it is: Olivia Kimball. Died two months ago.

"Well at least you found yourself," I say, expecting a laugh, but it doesn't come. I look at Olivia, pointing the light in her direction. And she's crying.

Crying.

"Olivia..." I have no idea what to do.

"Aaron, I wanna go home."

"You..." I start.

She falls to the ground, sobbing. I sit down next to

her, and awkwardly put my arm around her shoulders.

"It's okay. It's okay."

"You're lying," she sobs out.

Long pause, her sobs filling the silence. "It's gonna be okay. That much I can guarantee," I try smiling, and remember that she can't see me. "Let me get this hole dug, and we'll get you home."

I stand up, grab the shovel, and try as best I can to bring up as much dirt as possible, as quickly as possible. It takes me a long time. I don't check my phone and I don't look at my watch, so when I'm done I'm lost.

Olivia stands at the edge of the hole, looking down at me. I toss the shovel out, and I do my best to brush off the coffin I'm standing on and I pry the top open. Olivia is now next to me, and we peer in.

"Look at me," she whispers, kneeling down and touching her own sunken, burnt, decaying face. "I'm so broken."

All I can do is stand. Watch and observe.

There's a light coming from within the coffin. I can see the walls of dirt surrounding us clearly. I look back at Olivia as she stands up, and when she turns to look at me I can see her more vividly than I have since I met her. What shocks me more than any of this, even the light from the coffin, or the fact that I dug up a grave for a ghost, is that she is dissolving. Wisps of Olivia's body are pulling away, and streaming into the coffin. She looks back at me, a look of happiness across her face.

"Thank you Aaron." She's evaporating before me, dissolving into pure light.

She's gone and I'm alone. Standing in an almost pitch black grave, only I am present.

"Well there's no way I'm explaining *that* to anyone."

I fill in the hole, and I begin the trek back to my car.

Throwing the shovel in the trunk, and closing the door after I sit down, it's quiet. The clock says that it's five in the morning, and I drive home. Today was too weird for me to understand or even name, but I'm sure I'll remember it to my dying day. Or until I forget this life as well. Farewell fair weather. My apartment is cold and uninviting, and I don't have enough blankets to cover my sore limbs and protect them from chills. This December weather is atrocious. It's close enough to Christmas and the New Year to excite a normal person, but I haven't experienced either so it means nothing to me.

I welcome the cold into my life but it is not invited into my home, invading the space between cloth and skin, sending chills up my spine. My still-wounded leg feels awkward as I lie on the floor, staring at my bland ceiling.

CHAPTER TWENTY

Derek had odd taste in everything, and it seems I've inherited it. Living in Derek's shoes makes me wish for a few seconds that I knew him.

I sit quietly on the couch in my apartment. Seconds go by. Then minutes pass and hours fade away. The amount of time I've spent in here is ridiculous. I'm not even hungry. Sitting in the same position, my stomach doesn't growl, my muscles don't feel uncomfortable. I almost feel content. My front door opens and in walks Hayley and Sam.

Almost.

"Can we talk to you?" Sam asks.

"I guess," I say.

They walk forward, slowly. Hayley sits across from me in the comfy chair, and Sam sits on the couch next to me, separated by a cushion. They give each other odd glances.

"No Greg?" I ask, looking between the two.

"No Greg," says Hayley.

"We wanted to talk to you," says Sam.

"What about?" I wonder.

"You've been avoiding us," she says.

I pause before I say "So?"

"It's not good for you to be by yourself," she says.

"And you're here to change that?" I ask.

"We can help you readjust," says Hayley. "Get back into your old routine."

"No thanks, I think I'm good." My gaze lingers on Hayley for just a second more, wanting her to know what I think of her attempts to help me readjust.

"You need us," says Sam. "You need friends to help you when you need it."

"Do you think I need your help?" I snap.

"Yes I do. Especially after what happened. You can't just drift along by yourself."

"So far so good," I say.

"That's not how life works!" she says, leaning forward. "You need people to turn to when life is hard, and we're the people who have your best interests at heart."

I look at Hayley, glaring. "I don't think so."

"Aaron," says Sam.

"I don't need your help. I don't need anything."

Sam doesn't say anything. Hayley stands up. "Samantha, let me talk to you in the hall." Sam follows her and when Hayley opens the door, she steps to the side, letting Sam walk into the hallway, and Hayley closes the door behind her. I stand up, about to protest, but she's walking back towards me.

"Sit down, shut up, and listen," she says. I do.

"You were nice to me. You were serious, but you knew when to add some humor to make us more comfortable, which is something you did better than most people I know... You've got presence, and character. We notice when you're not there because it's painfully obvious. It's staring us in our faces. In *my* face. When we went to the viewing, and you straight up lied to the woman—it was like you were back. For one shining moment, Derek the

Funeral Crasher was reigning again."

I lean forward and look her straight in the eye.

"I'm not the king of *anything*. I'm messed up, I'm broken, I'm wasted, I'm a pair of lungs that can't be filled, I'm a voice that can't speak, I'm legs that can't stand, I'm arms that can't lift. I'm dead."

The tears have disappeared and now I'm just angry.

"Aaron—"

"I'm not Derek. I'm not even Aaron. I'm nameless. I'm a nobody. I'm the same as the girl that put me here. And despite all of this, it still feels like she understood me better than anyone else. There's no one alive like me, and there's nothing that they can do to fix me. And if they can't fix me, no one can."

Hayley steps back slowly, and she blinks a tear from her eyes.

"But the longer I'm here, the more I start to realize that maybe that's not such a bad thing."

She just looks at me.

"I'm sorry," she says, and she leaves.

I lean back on the couch. The end of an era.

CHAPTER TWENTY-ONE

I don't mind that Sam and Hayley came to talk to me, I mind that they ambushed me. My phone rings from over on the counter. Caller ID says Dr. Laien.

I pick up.

"Hello?"

"Derek? It's Dr. Laien."

"Yeah, it's me." I figure why get into the whole Derek/Aaron thing with my doctor?

"I just wanted to follow up on our phone call from the other day."

"Okay…"

"How are you feeling? Is your vision any better?"

"I'm feeling pretty good, and yes my eye is doing well," I say.

"Are you still seeing people?"

"No," I say, though I'm definitely not going to tell him why.

"Good!" he says. "I'm glad to hear it!"

But I freeze.

"Uh… yeah."

"Miss me?" Olivia asks, standing in my Living Room.

"Derek?" Dr. Laien asks.

"Uh huh."

"We were saying that it was good that you're vision has returned to normal."

Olivia waves at me with her fingers.

I try to bring myself back down to earth. "Er, yeah, it's very good."

"Was there anything else you were having problems with?"

"Not that I can think of," I say.

"Not with your leg or arm? How are they functioning?"

"Really well, actually."

"All normal?" he asks.

"Almost perfect, I've been pretty active lately." Yeah, I've been digging some pretty deep holes for myself.

"Excellent!" Dr. Laien says. "Keep on doing what you're doing, then, and give me a call if something bothers you."

"Sounds good," I say.

"Good-bye, Derek."

"Bye Dr. Laien," and I hastily hang up and look back at Olivia, still standing there.

"*What are you doing here?*" I hiss.

"Well I couldn't just be invisible all the time and I figured since you didn't want to hang out with your old friends that you could use your favorite new friend: me!"

She's excited.

"No, but, we— I dug up your grave and you disappeared! What happened?"

"I don't know. I thought I was going home, but

something was off. It didn't work," she says.

"That was the whole point of doing it!" I say. "*And* you said you'd leave me alone." I point my finger at her, accusing.

"I said in a perfect world," she says, sitting on my couch. "You can't deny that you're happy to see me. I'm the only one who doesn't want you to change!"

I stand still and look at her.

"I'm sorry it didn't work," I say.

"I had hoped it would work, of course. I guess I haven't solved that mystery."

"At least, not yet," I say.

"Thank you," she says. She gets up walks to the window. After a moment she turns around. "I want to show you something."

"What?"

"Where it happened," she says.

Olivia directs me as I drive and we park across the street.

We're both silent as I climb out of the car and walk toward the sad aftermath of destruction.

The space that once contained tables and chairs and people and a building is now wide and empty, the ground charred and dark stains on the ground remain where people laid; for the most part, the scene is still unchanged. Nothing restored. The restaurant that once stood here remains a sad half-shell, housing melted chairs and tables and condiments that no waitress will ever bus again. At least the dead have been bussed.

Sole Survivor. I'm still here. But I don't feel like I survived. I feel like I'm at the precise spot where I died.

Where, more accurately, Olivia killed me. I look down at my leg, and through my jeans the image of my marred leg is burned into my brain, the most obvious sign that I've been through Hell, even if I can't remember much of it. I sit. On the ground where the innocent bled and burned and felt fear for the last time in their lives. I didn't die. The biggest casualty for me was my memory. What does that make me?

That makes me different. It makes me noteworthy. It makes me wish I was dead because death is better than this monstrosity of an existence. Forget me. Think about the ones around me. Pity. A friend and a woman who miss the person I was, and a woman who doesn't understand who I am.

That's who I am. A special, different nobody. The same as everyone else. Feel sorry for me. Bring on the pity, because that's all there is now. A gimp that can't walk in a straight line. Bow down before me, because I'm a survivor. And I know this: My happiness is in my own hands. And I dropped it.

And. I. Know. This.

Sitting on the ground, growing angry at Olivia for putting me in this situation, she sits down next to me.

"Do you know why I'm showing you this?"

I shake my head.

"You needed to see what I did," she says. "People aren't perfect. And you never know what's going on inside of those people. You just never know." Her voice trails by the end.

"Did you really do all of this?" I ask, and she smiles.

"Come on," she says, standing up. "We should go."

When I get home I go into my bathroom and turn on

the shower and let it run. This is a comfort I have discovered in this depressing weather. I step into the shower and am embraced by the warm blanket of water and this is my first great love. The comfort of warmth in the days of darkness and cold. The water running down my skin, like rain, but infinitely better.

I normally spend these showers doing proper thinking. It is a place where interruption is unlikely, where thinking is encouraged. Where your mind can make sense of things. Where no one can ridicule you. Or you're just cold and need the warmth of a good shower.

I abhor the Winter cold, and with it the snow, wind, rain, and ice. The Winter that refuses to heat your faucet water so you end up washing your hands in the coldest water possible. The Winter that recommends you stay inside and in bed with a mass of blankets covering you, because if you venture outside you will freeze and never enjoy that warm bed again.

The number of people who have been blown up and then can't remember their past is a remarkably small list. And I'm at the top. You know why? Because most people who have been blown up, stay blown up.

The lesson here is to stay dead.

**

I have regained a very small collection of memories from my past, mostly obscure references to nothing in particular but that might one day come together as one to make sense, but nearly all the memories are scattered. The memories are unreliable, fleeting, emotional constructs that provide no true comfort. So this vision I have of myself, standing on a rooftop leaning in to kiss a woman, in reality – in the present – means nothing.

"You're gonna talk to her again?" asks Olivia, incredulous.

"Yeah," I say.

"*Why?*"

"I feel like it's something I should do."

"Are you going to talk to Greg? Hayley?"

"I haven't decided yet. I didn't have as much of an attachment to them as I did to Sam."

"This isn't going to go well," she says.

"I'm almost depending on it," I say. "Maybe it'll get her to move on."

"Best case scenario?" she asks.

"This." I'm confident.

"Wow you're an idiot."

A little less confident.

**

I sit down. She sits down. I force a smile. She smiles.

"Hi," she says.

"Hi," I say.

"So, back where we met."

"Here?" I ask.

"No, this is way nicer," says Sam. "We first ran into each other at a funeral."

"That's depressing."

"You're telling me," she says.

"Whose funeral was it?" I ask.

"A friend of a friend's."

"I wonder how I knew them," I say.

"Yeah," she says, looking down at the table.

"So, how are you?" I ask, trying to sound sympathetic.

"As well as I can be, I guess."

"That's good."

"Is it?" she asks, still looking down.

"It's better than being terrible," I say, shrugging.

"How are you?"

"I'm okay," I say.

"Just okay?" she challenges me.

"As well as I can be."

The corner of her mouth curves slightly.

"I have to mention something," she says, leaning forward.

"Okay."

"You call me, and you say that you want to get brunch?" she says.

"Is that bad?" I say.

"No man on the planet has ever asked another human to *brunch*."

"First time for everything," I say.

Our waitress walks over.

"Hey, my name's Lana I'll be your server this afternoon. Can I get you guys something to drink?"

"Whatever soda you have is fine," I say. Sam asks for coffee.

"Okay, I'll be right back with your drinks." And she's gone.

I turn to Sam.

She's staring at me.

"What?" I ask.

"I know you didn't ask me here to get back together, so why are we here?"

"I thought you might like to get together and talk."

"About what?" she asks.

"About anything. I didn't think our conversation would be limited."

"Okay," she says. "Is there anything specific you want to talk about?"

"I thought you might have some things to say, though I did have one question."

Sam looks down at the table, and then back at me.

"What did you see in me? What was so great about Derek that was worth marrying?"

She just looks at me.

"I'm serious," I say.

"You really want to go over that, right here, right now?" she asks, a bewildered look on her face.

"Yeah, I do."

"Fine," she says. "Compassion. It was clear you cared about yourself, but more so that you cared about other people. You were interesting. You held my attention even though you never asked for it. After we spent some time together, I could tell you were different from other men I've dated. You're not physical like they are."

"Did I not hold your hand?" I ask.

"You didn't hit me," she says bluntly.

"Oh."

"You cared about me. More than anyone else has. And that meant more than everything."

"And then the explosion, and everything changed."

Her eyes are tearing up.

"You weren't there anymore." She stops looking at me.

"I'm sorry."

"Why couldn't you have stayed the same?" she asks, her voice breaking.

"I don't know."

"Then who should we ask?"

I lean forward. "Look, I have absolutely nothing against you. I want for us to be friends. I really do. I don't think that's a far-fetched idea. Maybe I'm wrong, but I would like to try."

"Our wedding was supposed to be a week and a half ago, and you want me to be okay with what you just said?"

"Maybe not now, but someday. Things are rough for the both of us right now. When things calm down, and they eventually will, I want us to be proper friends, at the least."

"You seriously think we can just be friends?"

"I think it's possible," I say.

"You know," she muses, "I'd rather not put myself through that pain every single day."

"What?"

"Knowing you're there and this won't ever happen," she says. "I knew this was a bad idea."

"What was?"

"Coming here today. Good-bye Derek. Or Aaron, or whatever you're calling yourself."

She gets up from her chair and walks away, swinging her purse over her shoulder.

"I'll come back with the check," says Lana from right behind me, and I hear footsteps walking away.

"That probably could have gone better," I shrug.

CHAPTER TWENTY-TWO

There's a knock on my door so I go up and look through the peep hole.

It's Greg. I sigh and walk back to the kitchen and I pour myself a glass of water. His muffled voice sounds through the door.

"Aaron, it's Greg. Can I come in and talk to you?"

I consider it and drink most of my water before answering.

"It's open."

The door opens slowly and Greg walks in, cautious. He closes the door and then stands still, looking at me. I raise my glass towards him and ask "What can I help you with?"

He shifts his standing position, and says, "I just wanted to talk to you; see how you're doing."

"I'm good, thanks," I say flatly.

"That's good," he says.

I smile. "Yeah."

"So, uh, Christmas is coming up in a bit."

"That's right."

"Any plans?" he asks.

"I haven't settled on anything yet. The offers keep coming in."

"Oh yeah?"

"It's like trying to decide what gang to join."

He lets out a small chuckle. "Listen," he says. "I know we're not the strictest definition of friends, but this is important enough to tell you."

"Go for it," I say.

"I'm getting married," Greg says.

"Alright," I say. "Congratulations."

"Thank you," he says.

"So are you trying to keep me involved in your lives?" I ask.

"I thought you might like to come to the wedding," he says. "Bare minimum involvement."

"Okay," I say, nodding my head. "I'll think on it and get back to you."

"Good," he says, and he turns to leave.

"When did you get engaged?" I ask.

"Two days ago."

I give Greg credit for holding it in for so long. For some reason I was thinking he was girly about some things, and I figured this is something that he'd be shrieking about.

"Good job," I say.

He smiles. "Thanks," and he turns to leave but stops right at the door. "I know Hayley would want you there as well. I'll be waiting for your call."

"Thanks for stopping by," I say. I'm serious.

"Anytime," he says.

I finish my glass of water and walk to my office and turn on the computer. I open the word processor, and I write four words. Satisfied with these four, I write more.

And I write more. And by the time I go to bed, I have written five thousand words. This is the start of something new.

Merry Christmas to me.

CHAPTER TWENTY-THREE

Merry Christmas to me, in this skin that feels old and weary, with its scars. The only thing I've learned is the short-breathedness that time inspires, and how quickly things can go from bad to just ever-so-slightly better. The time that has passed since she was in my grasp isn't long, but it grows steadily longer. It ages, and that scares me. The fact that I age and time doesn't is terrifying, and I'll introduce you to the largest terror I have encountered in my renewed infancy: I. Will. Die.

Life will end, and time will continue without me as if I have done nothing in it. But time needs us. Time needs victims. Time needs me—now. But one day time will discard me and a new victim will arrive. A new challenge. Someone else to rip apart and tear from his threshold and his kingdom. Someone else will die.

Lather. Rinse. Repeat.

**

Hayley and Greg are getting married in a week. I'm the best man. Last night was the bachelor party. This sounds like the stupidest part of marriage, but since it was just Greg and myself, it was nice.

Scattered about in the apartment is a deck of cards, bottles of soda and alcohol, movie cases, and a lot of candy wrappers that Greg promised he would throw out.

So to recover from my long night in, I go out.

Sipping the last dregs of my coffee, I stand up and sling my bag over my shoulders. I walk across the courtyard to the trashcan to throw my cup away, but there's a man leaning against it. I glance around, and no other trashcan is in sight. No choice.

"Excuse me," I say, raising my cup towards the trashcan. His eyes grow wide as if I've scared him, and he jumps away from the can. I toss the cup in, and nod to the guy. "Thanks man." And I leave.

I walk down the block of this shopping center, moving in and out of the crowded sidewalk, and I notice by the reflection in the store windows that the trashcan guardian is following me. Speeding up just enough that he won't notice I'm scanning the side streets to see where I could go to lose this guy, but just as I'm planning my getaway I hear a voice.

"Hey."

I keep walking.

"*Hey!*"

I glance back over my shoulder, in case it's not that guy, but it *is* that guy.

"I really need to talk to you!" he calls.

I keep walking.

"I swear it's important!" he yells. "I need your help!"

I stop, and turn around to look at him as he approaches me. I think for a split-second that he looks oddly familiar to me as he studies my face, before he holds his hand up in front of me and waves it, looking surprised that I follow it with my gaze.

"What are you doing?" I ask, swatting his hand

away. "Stop that!"

"*Who are you?*" he asks.

"Who are *you*?" I ask.

He frowns, clearly disliking my response, but recovers.

"Lewis."

"What do you want, Lewis?" I demand.

"I need to know why you can see me," he says.

"Because you're standing in front of me," I say.

"No, it's more complicated than that."

The realization hits me like a bus.

"You're dead," I say.

"How did you know that?" he asks.

"You're not the first," I say.

"Really?" he asks, shocked.

"Really," I say. "So, you're dead. How long have you been dead?"

"A long time," he says.

"And why are you still here?"

"I've been trying to figure that out for a long time," he says.

"I might be able to help with that," I say.

"Really?" he asks, his eyes lighting up.

"Yeah," I say. "No promises, though."

"Where do we start?"

"We need to take a trip. There's someone you have

to meet."

Lewis follows me back all the way to my apartment and tries telling me a story about his past but I tell him to wait until we're settled in at our destination.

I have Lewis sit in my comfy chair and wait, and I sit on the couch with a glass of water in my hand.

"So," he says. "Who are we waiting for?"

"Someone who might be able to help you," I say.

Lewis laughs. "You know someone who can help me?" He holds his laugh, smiling wide.

I turn to look at him directly. "It's complicated."

He laughs even harder.

Olivia walks through the door and Lewis' laugh fades. She notices us sitting down, and notices Lewis looking at her and she slows down, her head tilted. I stand up and Lewis follows suit.

"Olivia, this is Lewis. He needs our help." He holds out his hand, and they shake.

"You're dead," she says softly.

"As a doornail," he replies.

She regains her composure quickly. "How can I help you?" she asks, more serious than I've ever seen.

"I'm stuck on earth. I need to get out of here."

"Okay," she says. "Sit down, and tell me everything you know. What's the first thing you remember?"

Lewis sits back down in the chair and Olivia and I sit on the couch.

Lewis looks down, trying to think, forehead creased.

"How did this start? Did you wake up in your coffin?" asks Olivia.

"No," he says, shaking his head slowly. "No, it was different." He looks up at us. "I was alone, and it was dark. Like I was in a large room, with no lights. Pitch black, I couldn't see anything. It was like that for ages. I don't know how long," he says, looking up at me.

"I walked around a lot. Going nowhere. Eventually I saw a light far away and I ran towards it. It grew bigger and bigger until I couldn't see anything but this brightness. Not blinding, but bright enough that I could see my hands. I couldn't see what I was walking on, but I could see my feet and the rest of my body. No floor, no ground. Just me, and the light. It was everywhere, and the light kind of, evaporated, and I was standing in a cemetery. There were so many people, all crowded around a grave. *My grave.* I saw her. Lori."

"Your wife?" Olivia asks.

He nods.

"But then she left," he continues. "My family; Gone."

"What did you do?"

"Exactly what you think I would have." he says. "I spent a lot of my time early on trying to contact Lori and get her to see me, or make her realize that I was right there. But—"

"Didn't work," Olivia finishes.

"Right."

"So what did you do?" she asks.

"I started to just wander around, waiting for something to change," he says. "I was starting to think that it wasn't going to."

"Did something change your mind?" I ask.

"I discovered something," he says, leaning forward.

"What might that be?"

"I went to the cemetery to look around and see other people visit."

"And?" I ask.

"My grave," he says, his mouth curling into a smile. "It—"

"It glows," Olivia finishes.

"Yeah," he says. "How did you know that?"

"So did mine," she says.

"It glows?" I ask. "Like there's a light and everything?"

"It was green, yeah," says Lewis.

"Was?" I ask.

"Mine was yellow," says Olivia.

"You didn't tell me that," I tell her.

"It doesn't keep glowing. It stopped by the time we went."

"But what does that mean?" I ask.

"I thought it meant that I had to touch it, or something, but nothing happened when I did," he says.

Olivia scratches her head, and I'm lost.

"What are you thinking?" I ask her.

"Can you show us?" Olivia asks him.

"Show us what?" I ask.

"If you drive, I can. It's a long way to walk," says

Lewis.

"Show us *what*?"

"Let's do it. Aaron?" Olivia says, turning her head to look at me.

"The grave? Really, we're there?" I ask. "Sure, why not? It's only taking directions from a ghost. Let's go."

**

The sun casts a steady, warm glow on us as Lewis walks briskly through the cemetery, Olivia right behind him wildly looking around, searching, and I trudge in tow, half paying attention. Lewis leads us up and down winding paths for at least five minutes before he says "There it is" and we leave the walkway and walk between rows and rows of headstones. The two finally stop and Olivia gives me a death stare as I catch up to them, lording over a plot with the name Lewis Jefferson on the headstone.

And suddenly I recognize him. A large print of Lewis' face with smaller photos attached to it and a crying woman, and Hayley and I running away.

"Here I am," he says.

"It's a good looking grave," says Olivia.

"Thanks."

"It's not glowing," I say flatly.

"I've been here for a while." Lewis says. "The light faded long ago."

We all stare at it.

"So what now?" I ask. "Do we say some magic words and poof you're home?"

"You said you'd help me," says Lewis.

"I said she could help you," I say. "What did you expect? You're dead! I'm not a wizard."

"Both of you, shut up!" Olivia says.

"What?" I ask.

"It could look a little suspicious, arguing with nothing." she says, looking at me sideways.

"What are you thinking?" I ask.

"I think I have an idea."

"Really?" Lewis asks excitedly.

"Do you remember what we tried for me?" she asks.

"Yeah, but it didn't work."

"We could try it again," she offers.

"Why would we do that?" I ask, taken aback.

"It might work for him."

"Why?" I ask.

"What is it? asks Lewis.

"We tried to send me away by re-burying me," says Olivia.

"That's it?"

"That's it," she says.

Lewis just stares at her.

"Sure, let's dig up the grave and shove him in," I say sarcastically. "Let's give it a shot!"

"Good," she says. "We have some planning to do."

"Planning? What's there to plan?" asks Lewis. "We can't just get some shovels and get this done now?"

"We don't have shovels," I say. "I borrowed them last time and I don't want to ask Greg again just for him to get suspicious and find out I'm digging up graves."

"And we can't just run to the store and come back," says Olivia. "It's not enough time. Plus the risk of being caught is too big. We'll have to come back."

She turns to Lewis. "Tomorrow night. Same time. Meet us here, and we'll take care of it."

"Alright. I'll take it," he says. "See you then."

The sun disappears behind the trees just as we watch him leave the cemetery.

I wait for him to round the corner before turning to Olivia.

"This is bad," I say.

"I wouldn't say it's bad. Inconvenient, maybe."

"You don't get it," I say. "I know him."

"You know him?" she asks, puzzled.

"Lewis Jefferson. I went to his viewing. I encountered his wife."

"Lori?" she asks.

"Yes, Lor – doesn't matter." I wave my hands as if I'm erasing the words in mid-air. "This is a problem!"

"I don't think so," she says. "We just have to get him out of here."

"It's worse than that," I say. "I have to tell Hayley."

"Why?"

"She can tell me if I'm crazy or not." I glance up at the darkened sky. "It'll have to wait until tomorrow to tell her. Come on, let's go."

CHAPTER TWENTY-FOUR

Olivia stands next to me outside Hayley's door as I knock. I had called Hayley right before lunch. I told her that I needed to see her. Just her. Olivia rode shotgun with me just in case.

Hayley opens the door and Olivia doesn't move, stiff; nervous.

"Hayley, hi!" I say, trying to seem like nothing's wrong.

"Aaron," she says, smiling. "It's been a while."

"Absolutely too long," I say.

"Come on in," she says, stepping back and holding her hand out.

The two of us walk in, and we all stand in the foyer. "Would you like to sit down?" Hayley asks. "Are you thirsty? I have some drinks."

"No thanks, I'm fine," I say.

"So what can I do for you? I was surprised you called." Hayley folds her arms.

"This is going to sound a little weird, but I need the obituary."

She doesn't move. "Are you sure?" she asks.

"Very."

"Does this mean...?"

"Something weird is going on, and I won't know anything for sure until I see it," I say.

"Something weird?" she laughs. "More than already?"

"I'm serious."

Her smile disappears. "Okay," she says. "Why don't you have a seat in there, and I'll go get it," She points to a room to our right, and she leaves.

I turn to Olivia. "Are you okay? You seem a little off."

"I think so," she says. "We should sit down." We walk into the room and sit on the couch next to the wall, with two single chairs sitting facing it. Hayley returns moments later with an envelope, hands it to me, and sits down opposite. It's marked *Aaron Foley. Just in case.*

"Thanks," I say, and I rip it open and remove a folded piece of newspaper. I let out a breath and unfold it. There, at the top of the slip is a picture of Lewis Jefferson. Olivia has a sharp intake of breath and I look back up at Hayley.

"That's definitely him," I say.

"What?" asks Hayley, unsure.

"I guess we have to tell her now," says Olivia.

"Okay, we have a problem," I say.

"What kind of problem?" asks Hayley.

"Like I said, this is very weird." I take a deep breath. "Lewis Jefferson is a ghost."

"You believe in ghosts?" she asks.

"I do now."

"Are you telling me that you've seen a ghost?" she asks.

"Well, yeah," I say, "I know it sounds stupid but—"

"I can't believe you're wasting my time with this," she says.

"I promise you I'm telling the truth," I say, leaning forward. "I wasn't able to see them until my eye started working again," and I point to it.

She looks at me. "What does the obituary have to do with it?"

"I needed to see his face to be sure."

"I still think you're full of it."

I don't say anything.

"I think you should tell her about me," Olivia suggests.

"Okay," I say. "Lewis isn't the first one."

"Is that so?"

"Her name is Olivia."

"Go on." Hayley waves an aggravated hand at me.

"She was killed in the same explosion that killed me." I decide to leave out the part where she caused it.

"Olivia what?" Hayley asks.

"What do you mean?"

"What's her last name?"

"Kimball," I say.

"Oh no," she says.

"What?" I ask.

"I need to get something," she says and leaves.

Olivia and I stand up and follow her through the hallway, past a door and down the stairs into the basement. Hayley is sifting through a solitary filing cabinet drawer on top of a desk, rustling papers.

"What is this room?" I ask, looking around. Next to the desk, which is drenched in papers, there are filing cabinets upon filing cabinets lining the walls all around the room.

"This is my office," she says, lifting a paper out of the drawer. "This is where I keep everything that Greg can never know about." She turns around. "But this is important." She reaches out and hands me the paper. It's another obituary, but it's for Olivia Kimball, with her picture at the top.

"No wonder she looked familiar," says Olivia. She's glaring at Hayley.

"Olivia," I say.

"What?" she asks.

"What if you're here because someone crashed your funeral?"

"She's here right now?" asks Hayley, her face losing all color.

"It would explain a good deal of this," says Olivia.

My legs begin to shake so I sit down on the floor. "You…" I say. "You crashed her funeral."

"Yes," Hayley breathes.

"We did this," I say quietly.

"If she's here because of me," says Hayley, wide eyed and white as a sheet. "Is Lewis here because of us?"

"He might be," I say. Hayley sits down too, and Olivia sits on the stairs, stony-faced.

"What can I do?" she asks.

"We don't know yet," I say. "We're going to try re-burying Lewis tonight, and hope it works."

"Maybe I should be there," she says.

"That could be a good idea," I say.

"What do you need for it?" she asks.

"Shovels," I say.

"Let's go, then." I look at Hayley. She's as serious as I've ever seen her. I look back at Olivia, and she nods.

"Okay," I say. "Let's go."

**

Pulling up the car to just before the mouth of the alley, I put it in park and step out of the car. I look up the block at the cemetery entrance and open the trunk.

"I still think you shouldn't have paid with a credit card," says Olivia.

"Too late now," I say, holding out a shovel to her.

"I can't carry that," she says, arms crossed.

"Can't you...?"

"Have I ever?" she asks, raising her eyebrows.

"Yes," I say. "When we met!"

"What?" she asks, and I can't tell if she's messing with me or not.

"You pushed me! You opened my front door!"

"Look, she's here," says Olivia, pointing. I turn to

look and there's a car pulling up behind us.

"Great," I say. I put the other shovels back in the trunk and slam it shut.

"You probably shouldn't be so loud," she offers.

"The kind of help I need from you isn't verbal," I say.

"It's all you're going to get," she says.

The car stops behind us. The lights dim and Hayley steps out.

"You made it," I say. "Good."

"I guess we'll see how this goes," she says. "I swear, if this is some stupid prank and this is all for nothing, I'm going to kill you."

"You won't have to worry about that," I say, hoping beyond hope that this works. "What did you tell Greg you were doing?"

"I told him I was going out."

"That's it?" I ask.

"He's good enough that he doesn't need to know what I'm doing every second of every day."

"That's good for us," I say, and I hand a shovel out to Hayley and she takes it.

We walk briskly to the front gate of the cemetery and Lewis is already there, waiting for us.

"Who's the new girl?" he asks rudely.

"This is Hayley," I say. "Hayley, this is Lewis," and I immediately feel stupid because she can't see him so in her eyes I'm motioning at a wall.

"Hey," he says.

"Hello," she says tentatively.

I nod, and Olivia says "Hello."

"Shall we go in?" asks Lewis excitedly, pointing his thumbs in the other direction.

"Might as well," I say. "Don't fall behind," I say to Hayley.

Trekking up the paths following Lewis since I have no idea how to get there, it's not long before he says "Over there" and leaves the path. Almost pitch black outside at this point, I set up a flashlight onto Lewis Jefferson's grave and toss the shovel on the ground.

"Who wants to start?" I ask, looking around. Hayley gives me a weird look. "Alright then, I will." I scoop up the shovel and stick it in the patchy grass above Lewis' body.

"I guess I'll help," says Hayley, and she joins in.

"Oh geez, this is nerve-wracking," he says quietly behind me.

"Yeah, I'm shaking," says Olivia.

"Is that sarcasm?" he asks.

"Absolutely," she replies. "But it is kind of exciting, isn't it?"

"And very tiring!" I grunt, hoisting dirt to the side.

We dig and dig and dig. I'm starting to regret saying I'd help.

Maybe a half hour later Lewis is leaning over the ditch we've made, and I just know he's about to say something that will annoy me.

"How far down are you?" he asks.

"The issue isn't how deep we are," I say between

flinging shovelfuls of dirt away. "The problem is making the hole wide enough that we can get to the whole coffin."

He doesn't say anything. I pause.

"Maybe four feet, at this point," I say, sighing.

"Ah, I see." He takes a step back. "Thanks."

I grunt a response and scoop more dirt out.

And then there's the muffled thud of metal connecting with wood. No one says anything. I hit it again, just to hear the sweet sound that tells me the finish line is in sight. Hayley and I look at each other. We do what we can to make the hole wider and after a few minutes I decide it's good enough and toss the shovel out, and Hayley climbs out too. I have to stand at an awkward position to attempt to access the coffin's edges but I'm able to grip it, and I pull.

It doesn't budge.

I pull again, harder.

Nothing.

"Hey Lewis?" I call out.

"Yeah?" he says back.

"Was your coffin nailed shut?" I'm gazing up into the night sky, blind to anything else. I don't hear anything. "What's that, Lewis? Was it?"

"I'm... I'm not sure."

I jump and clasp my hands on the top of the grave and hoist myself up, my legs kicking at the walls.

"I'm thinking it was," I say, standing up. "I'm not going to try to pry this thing open, so how about we try out little thing now?"

Olivia and Lewis look at each other.

"Worth a shot," she says, gesturing towards the grave.

Lewis steps forward, looking in. He looks back up. "What should I do?"

I look at Olivia, who's starting to look scared.

"I don't know," she says. "What do you think, Lewis?"

"Maybe I should climb down," he says, cautiously peering over the edge.

"It's your show," I say. I turn to Hayley. "Lewis is going to climb in and connect with the coffin. It's not quite re-burying, but it's the closest we're going to get."

She nods, but I'm sure she's still beyond confused.

"Okay, I'm going to do it," he says, and he shakes his arms and cocks his head from side to side. "Here goes nothing."

He kneels down and tries to lower himself slowly, but loses his grip and falls in with several thuds. Olivia and I rush forward and look in, and Hayley slowly follows us to the edge.

"Did it work?" she asks.

Thinking that it's probably a good thing Lewis is already dead, I ask him "How did it go?"

"It didn't work!" he says angrily. "It didn't work!" Lewis looks up at us. "You lied to me! You told me you'd get me home!"

"No," I say, putting my hands out in defense. "I told you we'd try to help. This was just one test—"

"What's going on?" asks Hayley.

"You lied!" he yells, his voice cracking. "You were supposed to—"

"He fell in, but it didn't work," I tell Hayley.

But I stop listening, distracted by the glow of a greenish light emanating from beneath his feet and I point towards it, stopping him mid-sentence.

The light intensifies, illuminating Lewis entirely, and shining off of our faces as we look at one another, astonished.

"It's working!" Lewis shouts, looking at his coffin and kneeling down to get closer to it. The light grows even more in response, and shoots upward, bringing with it such a force that it knocks Olivia, Hayley and myself falling back onto the ground so we're forced to gaze up at the sky, impossible to tell if the light has an end.

Electric lines shoot through the light, still green but distinguished, jagged and fast, appearing as swiftly as you blink. And as fast as it began, the light disappears and we're covered in darkness again.

Blinking quickly to try and regain my vision, I get up on my hands and kneels and do my best to crawl towards the grave again.

"What on earth was that?" cries Hayley somewhere on my left. "The lights, and that, that shove." She looks over at me. "What *was* that?"

"Lewis?" I call out. No response. Still blinking, I call again. "Lewis!"

"Lewis?" Olivia asks from above me, probably unaffected by the light.

The grave comes slowly into view, and I peer in. There's nothing. *Nothing*. No Lewis. No body. *No coffin*.

"Gone?" I mutter. "So-"

"It worked!" says Olivia, aghast.

"Did it?" I ask. "You came back, after all."

"No, this was something else."

The three of us stand over the hole together and peer in. Hayley takes a big breath in.

"Holy crap," she says, slowly.

"Wow." I bend my knees and fall down to sit.

"This episode is finally over," she says, sitting down beside me. "Not a moment too soon."

"A few moments too late, in my opinion. What a light show!" I marvel. Hayley whistles.

"That was incredible!" I exclaim, falling back and letting my head hit the ground.

"Weird. So," she says, rising to her feet. "It worked?"

"Yeah, it worked."

I open my eyes and turn my head, and I notice the large piles of dirt around me.

"So," says Hayley. "For Olivia, since I crashed her funeral, I should re-bury her, then?"

I look at Olivia. "What do you think?" I ask.

"I think I'll stick around a while longer," she says.

"She's going to hang around for a while," I tell Hayley.

"Alright then," she says.

"Do you think we can leave the grave as it is?" I ask, hopeful.

"I don't think so," says Hayley.

"Shame," I say. "Let's get to it, I guess."

Hayley picks up her shovel and scoops up a load of dirt.

CHAPTER TWENTY-FIVE

On Christmas morning I've put my comfy chair by the window and sit in it with a glass of water to wake me up. Olivia stands by the window with me, silent. I'm pretty sure Greg and Hayley are supposed to come over at some point. Gifts may be involved but we never talked about it. I didn't buy them anything.

I watch the gray sky pass and dissipate, making way for the sunlight. No one's on the street this early in the morning. Most people probably wouldn't be awake, but for their sleepless children.

"They're here," says Olivia.

"Here we go," I say.

My door opens and in walks Greg and Hayley, bags in their hands.

"Merry Christmas!" Greg calls.

"Do you have a key to my apartment?" I ask.

"For emergencies only!" says Hayley, placing bags on the counter and, running out of space, the floor.

"It's *Christmas*!" I say,

"What better emergency than seeing a friend?" she ponders.

"Actual emergencies!" I say. "Give me the key!" Greg tosses it at me. "Merry Christmas to you too."

"Wow what a Grinch," he says.

"And proud of it," I say. "What's in the bags?" I

ask, eying the collection on my counter.

"Presents!" Hayley squeals excitedly.

"We thought you could use a proper Christmas," says Greg.

"A little overenthusiastic, no?" says Olivia. She walks to the couch and sits on the end farthest away from me.

"I didn't know we were doing presents," I say.

"Oh that's okay, I gave myself some great stuff on behalf of you, And thank you for the new earrings, they're wonderful," she says, tossing her hair back so her jewelry shows.

"They're lovely," I say, holding back a smile.

"Among other things, one gift I have for you is breakfast. I hope you're hungry," says Greg.

"I'm getting there," I say.

"Good. Waffles all around!" he says, rubbing his hands together, and a wicked grin spreading across his face.

The first gift I receive is from Greg, a rare collectors edition of a movie he thinks that I'd like. Greg tears the wrapping off of his gifts in rapid succession to reveal the new gaming console (welcome to the next generation), a few films from the Criterion Collection, and a book I'd never heard of.

There are some unlabeled gifts, so none of us know who they're from, but they include a dress with shoes to match for Hayley, a set of sweaters that look warm for me, and a cookbook for Greg. Hayley gives Greg a kiss and an oddly lumpy sweater that I kind of like, which unfolds to reveal a brand new camera for Greg. I notice the tag on the box says "For Greg. And me. Mostly me." She gives me a sweater that I like more than Greg's, and a large bag of assorted chocolates—which will be enjoyed soon.

Greg sets about cooking this massive breakfast. Pancakes, scrambled eggs, bacon and sausage, hash browns. It smells amazing. While I examine the ins and outs of all my new toys, Hayley says she wants to make a pot of hot chocolate from scratch. She says it's a tradition.

We sit down and Greg bows his head.

"We thank you for the food that has been prepared, and we thank you for fellowship and the giving of gifts, and that we all could be here today. Amen."

And Greg is the first person to dive in and grab at least three strips of bacon, a stack of pancakes, and two sausage links.

"Oh no, no you don't," says Hayley. "Breakfast foul. Greedy people must wait until everyone has their first plate full in order to eat."

"That's not a thing," Greg says.

"It is now," says Hayley, who has not added any food to her plate yet, and though I've already filled my plate and started eating, she reaches forward with such laziness that Greg is drooling, just watching her slow-moving fingers.

"Come *on* Hayley," Greg says, eying her plate hungrily, and I can almost see the smell of food rising from her plate, floating by Greg's nostrils. I finish my first plate by the time Hayley fills her own and Greg can finally start to eat.

"I have never had to wait so long to eat my own food before," he says, his voice dry, but I know he doesn't care anymore now that he's fed. "That was *not* in the Christmas spirit, Hayley."

There isn't much conversation during our small feast, and I think this morning it's preferred. Simply enjoying each others company.

"So, what are the plans for the rest of today?" Hayley asks, in between bites.

"I've got nothing," I say.

"They're going to ambush you," says Olivia, and I cough.

"Well," says Greg. "We were thinking it might be a good idea to see your mother."

I set my fork and knife on my plate and sit back in my chair. "I can't say it's high on my action item list."

"It'd be very nice for her to see you," says Hayley. "She hasn't had any contact with you in weeks."

I don't say anything.

"Well you might as well!" says Olivia. "Who knows, it might be good for you."   I look at her. "No, I'm not going to go!" she says. "It's *your* weird family"

I sigh. "Alright, we'll go for a little bit."

"Good!" says Greg.

On our way to my Mother's house, I don't know how I feel about it. I know I should be with her more often, especially in my situation of being raised from the dead, but I haven't seen her since I was in the hospital. The drive is short and as we pull up to the suburban house with the perfectly-sculpted yard I grow nervous.

"How are you functioning so well after last night?" I whisper to Hayley as we walk up the driveway.

"I don't sleep much as it is," she says. "It was easy." She glances around. "Is Olivia here?"

"Not right now," I say. "She's off doing … what Olivia does, I guess."

Hayley gives a somber nod and we're behind Greg, who's knocking.

Mom greets us at the door with large hugs, even Hayley who she's only met once.

Love you too, Mom, I say, forcing a smile, and we take our coats off and everyone settles in.

"So how have you been, Aaron?" Mom asks, pulling me in for a hug and looking up at me, smiling, the rest of them already sitting down.

"I'm doing pretty well. Nothing to complain about," I say. There is silence for long time. Greg and Hayley are sitting on the love seat, keeping to themselves, suddenly interested in Hayley's engagement ring, and I'm simply there, sitting in a chair opposite. I figured this would be awkward, but this is more than I expected.

"I really love your decorations, Mrs. Wilson," Hayley says, looking up.

"Oh, thank you," my Mother replies, blushing.

A ding is heard from the kitchen, and my Mother bustles to rescue whatever food she's cooking from burning.

"I'll help," Hayley says, despite my Mother's protest, and they busy themselves setting the table and putting out drinks, etc.

I look around the room that I apparently spent my childhood in.

"Do you remember any of this?" Greg asks, standing next to me.

"No," I answer. This territory is foreign. Hayley laughs from the kitchen. Greg pats me on my arm. "Let's see what we can do in the kitchen," he says. We walk in and lend a hand putting the food into serving dishes and getting our own drinks because it turns out that Hayley has no idea what we all like to drink and if we're not happy with what we got we should all just get our own stupid drinks.

Other people start arriving. Family that I don't know and neighbors and friends who, it seems, have nowhere else to go. Everyone settles in with their plates of food.

I think I like Christmas.

Sitting next to my Mother, she leans in close to me while Greg and Hayley are standing by the counter, still getting their food.

"I'm glad you came," her voice is quiet, making sure only I can hear.

"Thanks Mom," I whisper back. "It's nice to see you." She reaches behind me and pats my back.

They've been kind all day. The food is great, although someone mentions that the food on Thanksgiving is better, and what do I mean when I say I don't remember Thanksgiving dinners?—and of course I've had pumpkin pie before, my Mother assures me. IKEA furniture, a table stocked with enough food for a family, not a problem in sight, hugs and kisses, Merry Christmas and Happy New Year and presents and a Mother who missed her sons, though she did voice her displeasure in Marshall's absence due to a new job in Philadelphia. This is the world I've entered. And I like it. Most of the meal is spent in mindless conversation about a politician who had some kind of scandal or how the weather is particularly cold this Winter, and, at one awkward moment, the process of getting one's tongue tattooed.

Hayley looks at me from across the table and glances to the door, signaling that it's time to go.

As the night closes we sit in my apartment and Greg puts on an action movie that takes place during Christmas, and then the sequel which also takes place during Christmas. When that movie ends it's nearing one in the morning and Hayley decides it's time to go home. Greg is staying here until the wedding.

"You made a good decision today," Greg says.

"Yeah," I say.

"Your mom appreciates you going to see her."

"I know."

"I'm gonna go get some dignity from the kitchen, you want anything?" Greg asks, rising from the couch.

"Just your pride," I say, tossing a pillow at him. He catches it, and chucks it back.

"I'll keep what God gave me, and God can take back what you don't seem to want," he says from the kitchen. He walks back to the couch. "Actually, keep your pride. I'm just gonna go to bed. I don't want to have a bunch of nights in a row where I stay up all night so I fall asleep at my own wedding."

And he walks away.

"Night, Greg," I say.

"G'night," he replies.

Silence. I go into my room and stare out the window at the lights beyond the glass, illuminating the small patches of world around them.

"You don't love her," Olivia says. I look at her. She's staring right into my eyes, into my soul, and I swear she's as real as anything I've ever seen.

"I don't love anyone," I say. I want to be heard.

"I know," she says.

"I thought it was just gonna be Lewis I'd have to

deal with this week."

"At least that one's over with."

"This feels pretty over, too."

"What does?" she asks.

"Like this is it," I say. "Like life is about to flatline while I'm standing in this apartment."

"It's just a quiet moment in your life. It'll pick up soon."

"It can't come any slower."

"Be patient," she says. "Be excited for Greg. Wedding's are a big deal."

"Yeah, I guess. I don't really care though."

"They're your friends."

"Because they have to be," I say.

"Is that such a bad thing?" she asks.

"I guess not," I say.

"Get it together. Don't ruin their wedding," she says. "You need them."

"Alright alright, I won't do anything drastic."

"Good," she says.

I close the door, and turn to look out the window again. "Good night," I say to the darkness.

"Merry Christmas," she says, dissolving into the shadows. I get into bed and close my eyes.

CHAPTER TWENTY-SIX

I'm about to start running water for a shower when I hear my phone ringing. Caller ID says Hayley.

"Hello?"

"Aaron, I had a thought," she says, sounding strained.

"Gee, I hope it's a good one," I say.

"I'm serious!" she says, urgently. "Remember when I said you collected obituaries?"

"Yeah?" I say.

"If Lewis and Olivia came back because their funerals were crashed..."

"Oh no."

"We could have some work to do," she says.

"Where did I keep them?" I ask. "Did I give them to you?"

"No, you kept them in your office."

I hang up and run to my office. My office isn't cluttered and almost all of my boxes are marked, so I skip most of them and head for the unmarked ones, thinking that would be prime placement for hiding secrets. I find nothing in the unmarked boxes, so I try *Taxes* next. Then *Bank Statements*. Then *Bills*. Nothing. I take out all the drawers from my desk and search them. Nothing.

"What could I have done with them?" I ask the room.

And then I remember. I gave a box of papers to Samantha. I had barely glanced inside before I handed them off. I pushed them onto her. I race out of my office and grab my keys and rush outside before I realize that I don't know where Sam lives. I get my phone out of my pocket and call Hayley.

"Aaron?"

"Sam has them."

"*What?*"

"I know! I gave her a box of papers, I thought they were scripts at first but the clippings must be in there too!"

"What are you going to do?"

"I have to try and ask for them back," I say.

"I could do it," she offers.

"No, don't. She'd never give them to you."

"Why would she give them to you?" she asks.

"I don't know. I have to try. What's her address?"

I hop in my car and slam the door shut, and I'm off. My stomach panics itself into a knot the closer I get to Samantha's house. Even worse knowing that I'm arriving unannounced.

I pull over across the street from her house and put the car in park.

"Looks like we're winging it."

I get out of the car and try to maintain an air of calmness as I walk up the drive to her front door. I take a deep breath and knock twice. I hear footsteps on the other side before the door opens, and there she is. She doesn't look happy to see me.

"Hi," I say, trying to sound pleased to see *her*.

"Why are you here?" she asks.

"I need your help."

"Oh, really?"

"Yes, and I promise it won't be for long, I just need something from you."

"How about 2 years back?" she demands, shifting her feet and putting a hand on her side.

This is going to be difficult.

"I can't give you any time back any more than you can give me my memory back," I say. "I tried to part on good terms but it didn't work."

"Thanks, Sherlock. I was wondering about that."

Let's try pleading.

"There are so many things that could have been done better, but I can't change that. But the reason I'm here is to try to help other people who need it. I do need your help in one last thing," and then I promise you won't ever have to see me again."

She looks at me for what feels like a long time.

"Fine. Get it over with." She stands to the side to let me in. "What do you want?"

"I need my box."

"Your box?" she asks, puzzled.

"My box that I gave you when I came home," I say.

"Let me go look." She walks down a hallway, and returns moments later with a packing box marked *Necessary*. She hands it to me and I set it on the floor. About to open it, I stop.

"Did you ever look through it?" I ask.

"No. Never could."

I open the lid and lying on top are the scripts.

"Your scripts?" she scoffs. "*That's* why you're here? Yes, I'm sure you'll help *so* many people with their acting careers. Have fun."

I peer further in and there in the dark are the yellowing newspaper clippings. I lift the scripts just enough for me to see. Satisfied, I close the box again and stand up.

"You don't understand," I say. "It's not about the scripts."

"Sure it's not. Why don't you go ahead and get out of my house?"

I look at her, knowing it's no use to say anything, and I shouldn't say anything anyway. I follow her advice and I leave.

In the car I call Hayley and tell her to meet me at the apartment.

I take the scripts out and toss them to the floor and I dump the newspaper clippings onto the dining room table, there must be at least hundred of them. Olivia stands silent by my side, watching.

"This is it," I say.

"It's so many," she says.

The front door opens and Hayley walks in.

"Where's Greg?" she asks.

"The movies," I say.

"Good, I was worried that he might—" she stops, noticing the table. She moves forward slowly, extending her arm and touching the clippings. "These are all ..." she says.

"Yes," I say.

She sifts through all the cutouts scattered on the table. "I knew it was a lot but I didn't know just how many."

"It's freaky," I say.

"So if we're right," she says. "All of these people are wandering out there, as ghosts?"

"Yeah." There's a lump in my throat the size of my fist.

"Probably not a good thing," she says."

"No kidding," Olivia chimes in. We just stand there, gawking.

"Do ya—" I pause. "Do you think I'm obligated to help them?"

"Yes," says Hayley.

"Maybe," says Olivia.

"Why maybe?" I ask her.

"How are you supposed to find them?" she asks. "Lewis was an accident—a chance meeting. You can't tell us apart from real people."

"I see," I mutter, thinking.

"What'd she say?" asks Hayley.

"It's be impossible to find them in order to help. They'd have to find me, I guess."

"I guess," she says.

"This isn't all bad though, right?" I ask.

"I don't know if I'd call it good," says Hayley.

"Oh, geez," I say, scratching my head.

"What?" she asks.

"Just think of all of *your* obituaries."

"Okay, this is definitely bad," she says.

"You guys are terrible people," says Olivia.

"Thank you very much for your input," I say. "Any time you want to go back, we'll make it happen."

"Absolutely not, this is getting good."

"Sticking around for the free show?" I snarl at her.

"Shame it doesn't come with dinner, too," she walks to the couch and plops herself down. "When you all come up with a solution, I'll be right here."

"She's being difficult," I mutter to Hayley who looks like she might go cross-eyed if this keeps up.

"So what do we do?" she asks.

"I guess we wait. Good thing I kept the shovels."

CHAPTER TWENTY-SEVEN

I wake up early. Six-thirty early. I lay in bed and try to think of nothing and coax myself back to sleep, but it doesn't work. I feel excited about today, even though it will not revolve around me in any way. It's the Saturday after Christmas and Greg and Hayley are getting married today. I get dressed quickly before making myself a bowl of cereal.

In the middle of lifting the spoon to my mouth I remember and I run to Greg's room and pound on the door.

"Wake up!" I call. "You're being evicted! Something about a woman, and money!" I pause. "And murder!"

The door opens slowly and Greg is standing there, hair lopsided, eyes half open, not wearing a shirt, his pajama pants backwards.

"You look lovely, my dear," I say, eying him up and down. "Come now, we must make you ready."

"Come back in a few hours," he mumbles.

"You get married in four."

"I *knew* there was something I had to do today," he yawns.

I push him back into his room and remind him that he needs to get dressed and that we still have plenty of things to do.

An hour later we've both had breakfast, showered, dressed, and are now sitting in front of the TV watching reruns of a show about a man who's been telling his kids a story for several years. We have no appointments until we arrive at the church for the festivities.

We pull into the church at ten thirty, park, retrieve our suit bags from the trunk, and make our way into the church. Inside, a woman directs us to an office that has a sheet draped from the ceiling in the corner. As we unzip the bags, I just stare at my suit. Greg pulls his out of the bag and lays it in sections on the large table in the middle of the room.

"Just look at it," he says. "Once I put this on, everything changes for me. For us. Our lives are going to be totally different from now on."

"I don't know what you think makes you a married man, but the suit is not it," I say. "Our lives will be different, but you've got another forty-five minutes as an unmarried man."

"I'm practically married."

"In the sense that you aren't dating another woman, yes. But in the sense of having a ring on your finger, and being in a commitment to God that you're going to be married to her for the rest of your life, no. That's a bright line, and you have not crossed it yet."

"But just look at it," he says, gesturing in exasperation to the jacket on the table.

"I know what the suit looks like," I say. "I picked it out." He disappears behind the sheet and starts dressing. I draw the shades over the windows, lock the door, and get dressed as well.

I look in the mirror and, for a moment, I don't know who is looking back at me. The man with his hair combed to one side, lint brush in hand, in a spotless suit and tie. I start feeling a little uncomfortable in my skin, so I mutter something about the bathroom and escape into the hallway. When I return to the office, I find Greg pacing the room.

"I'm anxious, and yet not anxious. Not quite nervous, more… excited," he's saying.

"That's a good thing," I say. I check my watch. Ten fifty-five. "Time to go. You ready?" He nods quickly. We walk out of the office and head to the vestibule, which is barely decorated for this small wedding.

"Go on then," I say, nudging Greg to walk up the aisle and wait in front of the pastor. A throat clears behind me and I turn. Hayley stands there with her single Maid of Honor, smiles all around, and the music starts playing faintly from the sanctuary.

Greg and I walk in and take our places at the front. The people in the chairs stand while the wedding march continues. I smile as everyone watches the bride make her way up the aisle.

The reception is at a local hall whose name I didn't catch. We're sitting at the table waiting for the host to let us know that we can eat, and I'm starving. My breakfast was small and long ago, and slipping farther back in time. I'm seated next to the maid of honor, and she says something about dissolving into thin air if she has to wait much longer. I like her already.

We wait fifteen minutes for Greg and Hayley to have their first dance, and for Hayley to dance with her father. Finally the "dinner" announcement, and I'm one of the first ones in line. It's a breakfast buffet. I've heard these were some of my favorite foods from before the explosion. Not much has changed in this area. French toast, waffles, bacon, sausage, and I will return for the pancakes.

Perhaps the most delicious food I've ever eaten.

People have started dancing to the modern club music, so I sit and talk with Greg for a while, and before long Hayley attempts to drag me onto the dance floor during a better song, so I oblige, Greg laughing as she pulls me away.

Greg disappears as we weave through the crowd on the dance floor, and Hayley just starts dancing, clearly having a good time. I stand still, people bumping into me and giving me a look.

"What's wrong with his *face*?"

"He looks terrible."

"Is he supposed to look like he just got out of prison?"

"I heard he killed his whole family."

"No, it was just his girlfriend."

"*That's* the best man?"

Hayley notices me staring into nothing and takes my hand and pulls me closer. She looks up at me, smiling.

"Words only have as much power as you let them. You weren't only brought back to Greg. You were brought back to me."

I look back at her.

"I'm so glad you're here with us." She pulls away and, still holding onto me, uses my hand as an anchor as she spins around and around, pulling herself back to me, and pushes me away and lets go. I collide with someone and as I turn to apologize, it's Greg who grabs my hand and starts spinning *me* around, drawing me in close and we start dancing. And we're having fun. I'm laughing like I haven't laughed in days, maybe weeks. Maybe since the explosion. The people around us have cleared the dance floor to make room for us goofing off. Greg spins out of my reach and he picks up Hayley and carries her in a wide circle around the dance floor, around me. He sets her down just as the song ends, and everyone starts clapping and moving in, past me, converging on Greg and Hayley. I back away and start walking back to my seat.

I sit down, loosening my tie, leaning back. Dancing isn't for me. Greg and Hayley have disappeared into the crowd and I start looking around the room, my eyes going from table to table, until my gaze rests on a bald man. Perhaps my age, but he looks weak and his skin is sunken. Probably seriously ill. The man's eyes are scanning the room, and as he turns his head he looks right at me. Right. At. Me. We stare at each other. He smiles. I blink and look away, staring into the dancing crowd. I glance back at the man, but all that remains is an empty chair. I turn back to the dancing people again and try to forget about him.

"Hi," a voice says, and I jump, looking behind me. It's him. "You alright?" he asks.

"I'm great," I say, relaxing in my seat. He sits down next to me. I notice he has an oxygen tank with him, though it's not connected to him.

"I'm Phil." He holds out his hand, which I shake warily. "You sure you're okay?"

"Yeah, I'm good," I say.

"Well your face says otherwise." I look at him. "Trust me. I'm good at knowing these things. You're worried."

"Nah, I'm all good," I say, but I know I sound fake. "Alright, a little bit."

"About what?"

"About me."

"Why?" he asks.

"Part of me feels that I'm losing my best friend."

"The guy?" he asks.

"The girl," I say.

"Why are you worried?"

"They're married now."

"What does that matter?"

"People are different when they're married. More time goes towards the other person, and less goes towards your old friends."

"I doubt that," he says. "I think you'll wind up spending even more time with both of them after this."

"We'll see," I say.

"Trust me, Derek."

"How do you know my name?"

"Your name is in front of you." He points at the name card in front of my plate. "Derek, something else is wrong, and you're not telling me."

"How do you know Greg?"

"I've never met him," he says.

"You don't know him. You're a friend of Hayley?"

"Nope."

"So you're crashing."

"Absolutely."

"Why?"

"I felt I should be here," he says.

I raise my eyebrows.

"Oh come on," he says. "Obviously I'm very sick. It's not hard to notice."

"Okay."

"Good."

A silent moment passes, and I look down at my name card.

The name on the card says Aaron.

"Here's what I think is wrong," he continues. "You're scared of life. You're scared of your old life catching up to you, and you're not ready for it. Your life has been scary, but you probably don't know enough about *living* to know what to do, so I'm gonna let you in on some advice:" he leans in, "—it goes on. Life continues no matter where you are or what you're doing. I know, my friend. I know. Life can punch you in the gut and kick you while you're down, but you have to get back on your feet and keep running, because otherwise life will leave you behind. Marry that girl. Take someone with you. You weren't meant to go through life alone."

"Where's *your* wife?" I ask.

"I didn't say it *had* to be a wife. I said you weren't meant to be alone."

"Are you alone?" I ask.

"I am very much alone. But I am at the end of my journey."

I scoff, and look back at the people dancing. He continues speaking.

"On the other hand, your journey has just begun, Derek."

"Stop calling me that," I say, turning back. But he's gone. "What the…"

Hayley comes back, "You've been sitting by yourself for three songs. Come dance one more with us!"

"What?" I ask, staring past her.

"I requested your favorite song."

"No, before that."

"You've been sitting by yourself for three whole songs," she says. I look right at her.

"No, I've been talking to someone."

"Who?" she asks.

I gesture to the empty seat beside me. "I, uh, I don't know."

"Was it a—?" she asks.

I turn back to her. "I have no idea who he was," She looks worried.

"What did he want?" she asks.

"He wanted me to – to be happy," I say.

"At least he's friendly," she says.

"Yeah," I say.

"Did Olivia see him?" she asks.

"She's not here."

"Hmm."

The song changes and it's more upbeat and not terrible.

"Come on, let's go dance," she says, holding out her hand.

We make our way to the floor, and the crowd swallows us up. Hayley and I, dancing poorly. Mostly I, but I don't care. We spin, and step two and three and four and I twirl her out of my arms, and she slips away, back to Greg.

I retreat from the dance floor and watch the other couples dance, enjoying my song playing over the loudspeakers.

And Mr. and Mrs. Greg Kailer walk over.

"The reception is just about over," Greg says. "So why don't you go home and I'll meet you there in a bit when I stop by to grab my stuff for tomorrow."

"Yeah that sounds good," I say. "I'll see you at home."

I arrive back at the apartment I now no longer share, and put on a movie. By the time it ends, the lights are dim. The sun's been set for at least an hour now.

I get up and walk to the bathroom and I start to get ready for bed. My jacket lays on the bed, shoes and socks scattered wherever I kicked them off; I take off my shirt and something catches my eye.

The scars on my body, the once charred skin that never fully healed, engraved in my side are reflected in the mirror that I avoid. I lean in and stare at my face, refusing to blink. I hate the scars. The blotch of what was burned. The jagged edge of slashed skin. I hate them.

Olivia comes into view behind me.

"Good wedding?"

"It was fine," I say. "They're happy."

"Good." Her eyes drift to my back.

She reaches out. "It's like art, almost."

"Not the word that came to my mind," I put my shirt back on. Olivia looks up at me. "It's nice that you like your own work."

"I'm sorry," she says.

"So am I," I say, blunt.

"I know you hurt."

"Why did you stay?" I ask. "You could have gone home."

"Because I've found something here worth staying for. There's nothing beyond for me."

"Here is better than there? That whole Heaven thing doesn't pique your interest?"

"I'll go eventually. For now I'd rather stay here."

"Why?" I demand.

"I can't help anyone whose life I took. I can help you."

"You didn't take my life? It sure feels like it."

"I changed you."

I turn and I'm inches from her face, making sure she remembers the words I say through clenched teeth. "You killed me. I just came back."

Hoping she'll go away if I leave it at that, I walk back into my bedroom, throw my clothes into the hamper, and turn off the main light.

"Hayley will always be your friend," says Olivia.

"I know," I say.

"You're moping like she's gone forever."

"I'm not worried about that," I say.

"You could have fooled me," she says under her breath.

"She is one of two people that I care about. Greg is fine – we're getting there. Hayley's the one who understands me. You of all people should sympathize with that. No, she's not going anywhere, but things will be different. We'll see if it's for the better."

The door opens and in comes Greg, followed by Hayley, and he walks to me. He embraces me in a wide hug.

"Thanks for being there today. It means the world to me."

"Glad I could be there," I reply.

"Lord knows you'd be there even if the world ended," Olivia says. Hayley comes and hugs me too.

"Our day was perfect, thanks to you," she says.

"I was just there," I say, shrugging slightly.

"And that was all we needed," she says.

They leave the room, and I leave too.

In the darkness I hear Olivia's voice. She whispers the name that had become a stranger to me, and suddenly I feel like I *am* Derek. No more Aaron. I am who I once was.

CHAPTER TWENTY-EIGHT

I'm slowly turning into the kind of person who re-alphabetizes their bookshelves, so that's what I'm doing today. I don't think Olivia appreciates it, since she's not involved and finds it boring, not to mention that she's been able to spend her time doing more important things. After the discovery of the obituaries we've been waiting for something to happen, to no avail. I don't know what we were expecting.

My discoveries of both Olivia and Lewis were accidental so our hopes aren't very high. This hasn't kept us from investigating, though.

Olivia walks in, hoists herself up to sit on my counter, and says "I've found them!"

"What?" I ask. This is the first sign of good news in the week since we buried Lewis. "All of them?"

"Just a handful. They hang out in the far side of the city," she says.

"Hang out?" I repeat. "Like, they live there?"

"Not in the strictest sense," she says, glaring at me.

"Sorry," I say quickly.

"They don't do much," she says. "They *can't* do much."

"Perfect opportunity for us, then."

"Exactly," she says.

"Did you talk to them?"

"Briefly," she says. "I told them that we may be

able to help them."

"So you could take me to them?" I ask.

"We can go now, if you'd like."

She guides me as I drive through the city until we come to a "T" intersection with a stop sign.

"Just over there," she says, pointing ahead. Past the perpendicular road in front of us is a steep decline leading to an aqueduct.

"Down there?" I ask.

"Down there," she replies.

We carefully slide down the sloping wall to the ground. "Which way?" I ask, looking left and right. She points to a shadowy area about a hundred feet away underneath a bridge where there seems to be three or four people milling about.

"After you," I say.

As we approach, the figures begin to move more and come out of the shadows toward us so I can see them more clearly, two men and a woman.

"She's back," one of them says.

Standing before us, in all their ghosted glory, they frown.

"This is the guy," says Olivia. "He's the only one who can help you."

"*That's* him?" asks the woman, skeptically.

"He *can* help us?" says the man on the left.

"Well, maybe," I say, holding up my hand. "If you guys come with me, I can show you how I might be able to help. Are there any more of you?"

"No, it's just us," he says.

"None at all?" I ask.

"Not that we've seen," says the woman.

"Well, I'll still try to help the three of you, if you'll let me," I say, looking hopeful.

They look at each other, and the man in the middle speaks up. "We'll come."

"Good. Now, before we do anything else, I'm going to need names."

"Alan."

"Monica."

"Jimmy."

I clap my hands together. "Good, let's go! Just up there, then." I gesture to where my car is and they follow me. It's a silent ride back to the apartment, but they came willingly which is all I can ask for.

I allow everyone into my apartment before myself, and as I close the door behind, the woman says "I remember having an apartment. Wasn't as nice as this one."

"Thanks," I say, moving past them to the dining room table. "Now, gather round, everyone." They do. "So here's the thing: You're ghosts, and you're stuck on earth, right?" They all nod. "And you have no idea why, right?" More nodding. "It's possible that I know the reason."

"Are you going to tell us?"

"See, the thing is, I used to crash funerals. It's what I did. And it's possible that because I crashed them, whoever died was unable to move on from earth. They're stuck."

"So it's your fault?" Jimmy asks.

"It might be my fault," I say. "It's... it's safe to assume that it's my fault. And no, I brought you here so that

I can help you move on."

"How are you going to do that?" asks Monica.

"Well look on the table here: lots of newspaper obituaries. If I crashed your funeral, you'll find your obituary."

"Are you serious?" asks Monica.

"Completely," I say.

They start digging through and within minutes, Alan says "Here's mine!"

"Good!" I say. Alan moves to the counter and stares at his obituary, frowning.

"Wow this is depressing," he says.

"Ain't it, though?" says Olivia.

"So you're, what? The sidekick?" Alan asks, eyes narrow.

"Before you talk down to me, you might want to remember that I'm the one that found you," she replies, and walks over to stand next to me. Soon Monica finds her own obituary, and Jimmy finds his.

"Okay, good, everyone's here," I say.

"So how does this help us?" asks Jimmy.

"Because I'm the one who crashed your funeral, it's probable that I'm the only one who can get you back. The next thing I need to know is where you were buried."

"Rockcliffe Cemetery," says Jimmy.

"Petersville," says Monica.

"Me too," says Alan.

"Okay, not too difficult," I say. "Do you know exactly where your grave is?"

They all say "yes."

"So here's what we're going to do: we're going to dig up your graves."

"*What?*" says Monica, shocked.

"In order for you to leave earth, you have to physically touch your coffin," says Olivia.

"You're kidding, right?" asks Jimmy.

"We've done it before," I say. "We've got the materials we need; shovels, you three. We're good. We just need to decide who goes first, and that will be the end of it."

"When can we go back?" asks Alan quietly.

"We could possibly do it tonight, but it'd be close," I say. "It's almost dusk."

"So let's get going then," he says, and looks at Monica and Jimmy, who hesitate, but nod.

"Alright," I say. "Who wants to go first?"

No one moves at first, but Jimmy tentatively raises his hand. "I'll do it," he says.

"Okay. We'll do it tonight."

**

I call Hayley on the phone.

"Hayley, we've got another one."

"Are you sure?" she asks.

"Actually, three, but we're only doing one this time."

"*Three?*"

"Yeah, but we're only burying one right now," I repeat. "Rockcliffe."

"Why just one?" she asks.

"Because he's the only one buried here. Meet us there at sunset, okay?"

"I'll be there." And we hang up.

I carry the shovels to the car and we all pile in; Olivia in the front with me, and the others in the back. I don't ask if ghosts can get cramped.

Hayley's already there when we pull up, leaning against her car. I stop the car and Olivia and I get out, the other three slowly following.

"What's this one's name?" asks Hayley.

"Jimmy is his name," I say. "Monica and Alan are the others. They're all here."

"Nice to meet them, wherever they're standing," she says.

"Yeah. Everyone, this is Hayley," I gesture. "Hayley isn't like me, so she can't see or hear you. But she's on our side. She's here to help."

They nod, silent.

"They say 'Cool'," I say to Hayley. "It's weird to know that there's six of us standing here, but you can only see me," I say.

"You're telling me," she says. "Are you ready?"

"Yeah, I think so," I say. I turn to face the others. "The plan is to walk in there, Jimmy will lead us to his plot, and Hayley and I will dig."

"Seems simple enough," says Alan.

"Couldn't be simpler," says Olivia.

"It could be," says Alan.

"Are we ready?" I ask, looking at Jimmy.

"Yeah. Yeah, I think so," he says.

"Good." I turn to Hayley. "Let's walk." We stroll across the street into the cemetery and walk in.

"After you," I say to Jimmy, holding my arm out down the path. He shuffles forward, clears his throat, and moves forward. I look at Olivia and raise my eyebrows.

"Here we go," I mutter.

"Down the rabbit hole," she says.

We walk for probably fifteen minutes before we leave the path and weave in and out of headstones to stop at a flat grave marker.

"I've always liked these," says Hayley. "They're simple but still look nice."

We all look at her. She meets my gaze, realizing what she said.

"Right," she says. "Sorry, Jimmy."

"No offense meant, Jimmy," I offer.

"None taken, I guess," he says, and looks back at the headstone. "Well, this is it."

"Yeah," I say. "Ready to dig?" I ask Hayley.

She nods. I take my shovel in both hands, look around to see if anyone is watching, and start to dig. Jimmy has an anxious look on his face. Alan and Monica both standing with their arms folded.

Seemingly hours have passed since we walked into the cemetery earlier tonight, and it's impossible for me to know how much time has actually gone by because it's so dark out now, but it's Hayley who hits solid wood first.

"Good job!" I say, and we squat down in awkward positions to clear away most of the dirt. I stand back up and claw my way out. I brush myself off and look at Jimmy. "Are you ready?" I ask.

He says nothing, but nods his head slowly.

"It's your show," I say.

"I just have to jump in?" he asks, his voice quiet.

"And touch your coffin," says Olivia.

"What she said," I say.

"What?" asks Hayley, utterly confused.

"He's good to go," I explain. She blinks at me. "Don't worry about it, just watch," I say.

Jimmy takes a step forward and sits on the edge of his grave, waits a moment to take a deep breath, as if about to dive underwater, and pushes off, landing on his coffin, knees bent. He stands up a moment later, and looks around. "Nothing happened."

"Try touching it with your hands," I suggest. He does so, pressing his palm flat on the wood, almost shoving.

Holding our breath, and I'm bracing myself for the bright lights and the push that's almost sure to come, but nothing happens.

"Well?" asks Alan from behind me.

"It worked last time!" I bark.

"Shut up, both of you," says Olivia. "There," and she points. A red light glows underneath Jimmy's shoes, faint, but growing brighter with every second, soon engulfing Jimmy and shining off our faces, culminating in a beam that rockets into the sky in an instant, knocking us all back with such force that it disorients us, unaware of who went where, and I'm transfixed, staring up at the beam and the jagged electricity wrapping around it. And then its gone, leaving us blinded in its absence.

"Still amazing," I say, still on the ground, keeping my eyes closed to stare at the picture burned into my eyelids.

"You'll have to draw me a picture later," says Hayley.

"Still uncomfortable," says Olivia.

"Jimmy!" Monica yells, and I turn to look. She's standing over the grave, Alan coming up next to her. "He's gone."

"It worked," says Alan.

"Like we said, couldn't be simpler," I say.

"When can we be buried?" Monica asks excitedly.

"The sooner the better," adds Alan.

"How soon can we bury them?" I ask Hayley.

"Tomorrow?" she says.

I look at them and look at them, eyebrows raised. They nod. "Tomorrow it is," I say. "Let's get this hole filled in and get out of here."

CHAPTER TWENTY-NINE

The following day I decide to visit the cemetery, alone. Olivia elects to wander the city in search of more wandering souls, so I'm walking up the smooth path by myself, passing each row, and trying to remember the last day of my previous life: what caused me to be here, what I was thinking, why I left, if I was angry or sad, or just wanted to see my Dad again. I stopped in the cemetery office and wrote down where the grave is. I finally find him between a tall statue of a saint I've never heard of and a headstone that I think says Peck but has been vandalized. I study the words on the headstone, hoping against hope that this will trigger my memories. I sit on the ground and fold my legs.

"Hi Dad," I say. "It's me. Derek. I think you remember me, even if I only barely remember what you look like. Just wanted to, kind of, conduct a test. Trying to see if some of my memory will come back by revisiting some important places. It's worked a little bit, but there are still pretty big chunks that are gone." I wait, but there's no reply. "But I guess that's not going to happen. Thought I'd give it a shot."

"What am I even doing here?" I ask the cemetery. "This is stupid." I get up, and walk down another path. "Yeah, I'll just go to the cemetery and my memory will just come galloping back. Obvious, right?"

"I guess I've just been lazy about missing my old life. But you can't miss what you never had, can you? Yeah, Dad, this was definitely worth my time." I make my way to the front gate a hundred feet away.

I cut through the grass and wind up stumbling on a

flat headstone, landing on my back. I cough, and lay there.

"Real funny, Dad." I close my eyes for a bit, and sigh.

I open my eyes, and the sun is setting.

"I think you're looking at this from the wrong perspective," a voice says. I look around, and the sick man from Greg's wedding reception is sitting on the headstone next to me.

"What?"

"You're angry at your Father for leaving. Why?"

"Why are you here?" I ask.

"Answer the question Derek."

"Why?"

"Because you're thinking about it. Might as well say it out loud."

I just look at him for a moment, then I stand up and open my mouth to speak and for a moment the words don't come. And then they all come at once.

"He should have stuck around. My life is changing, and who am I supposed to talk to about it? Isn't that what dads are for? Giving advice when I need it?"

"Sure. But you're angry he's not here? Explain that."

"What else am I supposed to feel?"

"Happiness."

"Happiness? Are you on drugs?"

"Not anymore," he says, completely serious. "Perhaps be happy that your Father doesn't have to feel any of the pains of this world. Happy that he's no longer ailing. No more daily pains. No more troubles. He's in a much happier place now, and you should be happy about that."

"But I'm here and miserable," I say.

"Miserable because you have two best friends who are expecting a child, and they're willing to go to the moon and back for you?"

I don't say anything.

"Miserable because you have a friend that only can talk to you?" he asks.

"What did you just say?" I ask.

"Sounds kind of silly now, doesn't it?" he continues. "Life is supposed to change. We're supposed to grow, and change with it. Instead of looking at life like it's throwing nothing but curve balls, maybe take a look at the scoreboard and realize that you're ahead of the game." He pauses. "The bases are loaded. You may think you're about to strike out, but a home run is always possible." He gets up and starts to walk away, and I notice that he doesn't have the oxygen tank with him. He's not limping either. He's walking freely.

"Hey, where's your—?" I start to ask.

He turns back to look at me. "I don't need it anymore. I'm in a much happier place now."

"Who are you?"

"Just someone with some life experience. He thought you could use it."

"He?" I ask.

He just smiles.

I blink, and he's gone.

Hayley meets the rest of us outside my apartment and we go to Petersville in one car, but it's already dark when we arrive.

Petersville Cemetery is surrounded by a tall chain

link fence, and nothing else. Given the circumstances, we decide it's better to park behind the cemetery, climb over the fence, and proceed from there. Alan and Monica lead the way, Hayley and I sneaking behind. Her face masked in shadows, impossible to read.

Within minutes we've found Alan's grave. A tall pointed headstone, with a long inscription running from top to bottom.

"Let's get started," says Hayley. I squint at the ground as she digs her shovel into the dirt.

So we dig.

The dirt is loose and easy to dig out so that even though it might have been two hours for the two of us, it doesn't feel like it. I rest my knees on the casket and shove away as much excess dirt as possible, and Hayley's already climbing out. She gives me a hand up and I sit on the grass, breathless; Hayley, with all the grace of cow, lies down. Alan's just standing there, looking in.

"So, uh, this is it?" His voice shakes.

"This is it," I say. "The big one."

"Is he going?" asks Hayley from the ground.

"Are you ready?" asks Monica.

"I think so," says Alan, stronger now.

"He's going," I say.

"Good luck, Alan," says Hayley. "Don't be offended if I don't get up, I'm just going to lay here for a bit."

Alan cracks a smile, and turns to hug Monica. They let go of each other and he steps forward to the edge of the grave, and steps in.

The usual silence arrives and lingers for a few seconds, before the grave begins to glow blue, getting brighter and brighter from within itself before it blasts into the sky, the blue piercing my eyelids as I'm forced to lay on the ground blinking furiously to gaze again at the light. I finally force my eyelids open but by now the light is faded and gone.

"Figures," I say. Monica peers into the grave and, upon finding nothing, sits back down.

"That's it, I guess," she says.

"For now," I say. "We've got one more before the night's over."

It takes us almost an hour to fill in the hole, and it must be midnight by the time Monica leads us to her own plot, the moon illuminating our path. She slows and points to a mausoleum. "That one."

We get closer and the first thing I notice is how dirty it is. Weather beaten and uncared for. I look over at Monica, and she's stony-faced.

"Last one," I say. Hayley looks at me and nods.

I walk up to the door and push against the cold metal. It doesn't budge. I put my shoulder against it and push harder. Nothing. Hayley comes up and starts pushing too, but it remains unmoved.

"One more!" I spit through my teeth, and we push with everything we've got.

It remains still. Hayley and I take a step back, our breathing rushed and irregular.

"Wait," Monica says, and I look at her. "Maybe I could go through it."

My single bark of laughter sounds flustered and weak. "Why didn't we do that the first time?" I ask the cemetery. "She'll just walk through it," I tell Hayley when she looks quizzically at me.

"Let's do that," she breathes.

I look back at Monica. "It's that time," I say, my haggard voice sounding much less impressive than I hoped. Monica looks right at me.

"Thank you." And she walks forward, pausing in front of the door, and steps through it.

I look at Hayley. "We should get down."

I sit and look back at the door just in time to see the purple glow emanate from the cracks between the door and the wall and exploding forth, breaking through the cement of the mausoleum with an ear-splitting crunch, and then nothing.

"That was very different from the others," says Hayley.

"You're telling me," I say. "Look at the damage that did." I get up and walk towards it. "It seriously damaged the place."

"Wow," she says, leaning in close to inspect it.

"I'm going to say that we don't have to clean this one up," I say.

"I agree, let's get out of here."

**

We pull up outside my apartment where Hayley had parked, and I climb out of the car and head for the trunk to open it.

"Oh no," says Hayley from the passengers side,

- 207 -

staring at her phone. She turns it to show me.

"What?" I ask, squinting at the bright screen. It shows nine text messages and several missed calls.

"They're from Greg," she says. "He's wondering where I am."

"What time is it now?" I ask.

"Late."

"Is he normally like that?"

"Not usually," she says. "The last message says 'See you tomorrow.' That's a good sign, though." She looks at me. "Right?"

"I'd think so," I say. "Are you going to text him back, or call?"

"Not right now. He's probably sleeping."

"Right. Can you help me with these, then?" I ask, gesturing to the shovels.

"Sure," she says, and walks over. We carry the shovels together up to my apartment and I let her in first, following behind.

"That was a long night," I say, maneuvering my shovel so I can better close the door. "Do you want to go home or would you rather sleep on the couch?" I turn around, lean the shovel against the wall and Greg's just a few feet away, sitting on my couch.

"I was meaning to talk to you, Derek, and see if you could answer some questions for me, but the subject matter involves both of you, so this will do just fine." He's staring at Hayley, who's white as a sheet. "Hello, sweetheart. Busy night?"

"We were—" she starts.

"Burying people, if this is true." He holds up a

small notebook.

"My journal?" asks Hayley.

"That's correct, and before I get any of the invasion of privacy jargon, I know, and I'm sorry and will explain, if you'll let me." He pauses, and continues when Hayley doesn't say anything. "I was cleaning our bedroom earlier tonight and when I got to your desk my curiosity got the better of me and I opened it. I am wrong, and I am sorry, and I am very curious as to just what is going on. Does anyone care to explain?"

We're silent, petrified.

He holds the book open, clears his throat, and starts to read.

"February 16th

Derek called me and said that he's found more phantoms. 3 of them, this time, and he wants me there to bury them. Olivia won't be joining us this time, though, to see if she can find any more. We're burying the first one tonight. I'll update soon. Hayley."'

Greg looks back at us, almost lazily. "I was hoping this was a book. A new creative project that you were working on. But I don't think it is." He stands up. "So, if you're telling the truth about what is in this book, it's a tragic miracle; you helping the people you've hurt, and Hayley for some reason can't see what you see."

Tears are starting to form at the corners of Hayley's eyes, but she's still motionless.

"Or," he steps forward, slowly, menacing. "Or, you're insane, and you think you're seeing ghosts, and you've duped my wife into following your crazy misadventures. That's what I think. Am I getting it right, so far?"

"Greg," says Hayley, and his eyes snap to her. "You have to hear it from Derek."

"Oh I will, I can promise you that. But after that, he's going to have to answer to a professional."

"*What?*" I ask.

"I never knew if you were really damaged, mentally, but a psychiatrist would love to hear these stories of yours."

"*Greg!*" gasps Hayley.

"He's lying to you, Hayley! Listen to what I'm saying! He's crazy!"

She doesn't say anything. Greg turns to me. "This is over. You're not going to hear from us any more, and we're leaving."

He grabs her hand and walks past me to the door.

"It's the truth!" I say, stopping the door with my hand. "I can see them. They're ghosts, and they're trapped here because of me! It's my eye! That's why I can see them. My vision is insane, and I can see and hear them and talk to them."

Greg yanks the door back, pushing me away, and hurries out.

"You have to believe me Greg! Don't do this!"

He stops and turns to me. "*You're* doing this!" he spits out. "You have no one to blame but yourself!"

Hayley's face is wet from sobbing and she's yanked away by Greg. By the time I regain my balance, the elevator doors are closed and I jam my finger on the button to call another. It comes, noisily, and dings open. I hit the lobby button and impatiently wait the seconds it takes to reach the bottom floor. By the time I'm in the lobby I see Hayley reluctantly climbing into the passenger seat of her car and I start to think I'm too late as they peel away, Hayley looking back at me and I think she's trying to say something but I can't tell. I can still catch them, so I'm rushing after them, stopped at a red light up the block. But the light turns green and I slow down watching them drive away again, and I hear the loud screaming of tires before I see another car come into view and connect with Greg's car like a thunder clap and the banging of a rolling frame followed by the deafening screech of metal sliding on the ground.

"No!" I'm screaming, and I'm running as fast as my body allows, my breath ragged and raspy.

I run past the car that caused the crash, it's front mashed in on itself. Greg's car rests on the drivers side and lying on the ground between the car and myself is Hayley, her limbs sprawled in an awkward position. I kneel down beside her and see her face, covered in a dark liquid, and unresponsive to my touch. "Hayley," I say. "Hayley, come on, wake up." Nothing. "Come on, Hayley, open your eyes! Open your eyes!" I'm repeating over and over again.

People are starting to appear in the windows of their houses and in their doorways and I'm yelling at them to call an ambulance.

"Call a doctor! Someone do something!" I'm screaming at them. Some get their phones, but others just ask questions from their safe places.

"Is she okay?"

"Is there someone in there?"

Greg. I sloppily get to my feet and walk to the car, sitting on its side amidst scattered broken glass and I peer in through the cracked windshield. Greg lies there against his window, crumpled, with a messy web of blood across his face.

"Greg!" I say. "Greg, can you hear me?"

People have started gathering around and inspecting the other car carefully.

"He's alive!" they're saying, but I don't care.

"Ambulance is on it's way!" someone calls over to me.

"Greg, wake up. Come on, open your eyes, do something!"

His eyes move, and they open a moment later.

"Good! Okay, you're okay. We're fine," I'm saying. "It's going to be fine. The ambulance will be here soon and it'll be just fine."

Blood dribbles from his mouth but I don't want to look so I stand up again and look around at the wreckage. The other guy is out of his car and resting against the side, holding his hand to his head. I start to walk over just as red lights are flashing around me, and I grab him by the shirt and get right in his face and yell.

"Do you know what you've just done? What you've taken away from me?" I scream. I scream louder, right in his dark eyes, wide and terrified, his hands raised to protect himself. "Do you know who she is? Who she..?"

Who she was.

He sobs, "I'm so sorry."

He cries, "I'm so sorry."

"The car pulled out so fast and I couldn't slow down... I'm sorry."

Hands are grabbing me and pull me away. Pulled me apart from my resolve. Firemen have showed up and are deadset on keeping me from attacking this man.

"Do you know what you've just done?" I ask again, defeated, broken, my life missing chapters, yet unwritten; my hands at my side.

There's a loud crash as the firemen get into Greg's car and begin trying to get him out.

Paramedics wheel a gurney past me, the large black bag resting on it, and I watch it leave. They load the gurney into the ambulance, and I feel a part of me leave.

I sit down on the ground, terror-stricken about what's to come. Greg is lifted onto a stretcher and carried to another ambulance.

"Can I go with him?" I ask a paramedic. He shakes his head, so I go back to my car and follow the ambulance as best I can.

**

I have to sit in the waiting room for a long time because Greg isn't processed yet, or something. It was hard to understand what they were talking about, so I decide to read Hayley's journal. Not wishing to read the latest entry, I turn back a page. A week ago.

February 11th.

Well, I've got some news for you. What I thought was food poisoning turned out to be a little nugget. That's what I'm gonna call him. Or her. I haven't told Greg yet. When he lays his eyes on this little plastic stick, he's going to freak out... But I think that's okay since I'm a little freaked out too. I mean, this soon? It's almost unheard of! At least if Greg freaks out he'll be in good company!

Derek seems to be doing better. He's been busy with this new task of his, but I think his spirits are high. I still worry about him, though. It's hard not to. Even Greg does, and usually the most he worries about is how much cheese we have for his steak subs. Speak of the devil.. he's here. I'll check in soon!

~Hayley

I've never lost anyone before. Just my Dad, and I wasn't really around when he died. Hayley is the first person I've truly lost. There's no lost and found for death. But, it's not just that Greg lost a wife; he lost his family.

A nurse tells me that Greg is in need of emergency surgery and waiting hours are over so I might as well go home and they'll call me when he can have visitors. I tell them that I can wait.

She says "Just go home."

I wake up the next morning and make myself get out of bed, even though my eyes are barely functioning.

"How did you sleep? I decided not to wake you." Olivia asks from the couch.

"Poorly," I say, walking to the comfy chair. "What time is it?"

"About noon," she says.

I grunt. "How long have you been here?"

"Long enough that I saw them cleaning up the wreck outside. I know that it was her car."

I nod, my eyes closed.

"Are you okay?" she asks.

I shrug.

"How's Greg taking it?" she asks.

"He's still unconscious."

"He's in for a rough time," she says.

"He's *in* a rough time," I say.

"Life was starting to be kind to me," I say. "Then it got hit with a car."

"I don't know if life was meant to be kind," she says. "Life was meant to make us stronger."

"My best friend is dead because of me."

"You needed her help, and she willingly gave it. Hayley didn't even understand what was going on, I'm sure, but she trusted that you knew what you were doing, and there's nothing wrong with that. But things don't always work out in our favor."

"Yeah Hayley's death is definitely not in my favor," I say, rolling my eyes. And then I remember. "Oh, Olivia."

"It's coming back to you, huh?" she asks.

"I'm so sorry."

"It's fine," she says. "I did tell her that I wanted to stick around."

"With the impression that you'd like to go back at some point!"

"Everything that happens to us is a chance to learn," she says quietly, like an adage she had been taught.

"What's the lesson, then?"

"I don't know," she says, looking at the floor.

"No?"

"I said it was a chance to learn, not that I knew what the lesson was."

"I'll try to think of something," I say.

She smiles, but the smile doesn't reach her eyes. "It's a nice thought, but I don't think there's much that could be done."

CHAPTER THIRTY

That night I'm sitting on my couch, now white, and my white walls reflecting the lights around me. Sitting on this white couch, in this white room, hands folded in my lap, and looking at me from the comfy chair, is Hayley. She's staring, not blinking, hardly moving.

"Hi," she says, and she smiles.

"Hey," I say. In the back of my head I know she's dead, but I'm not startled by the fact that she's here without a funeral or anything.

"Tough day?" she asks, frowning.

"Pretty tough," I say. "I'm curious, how—?"

"How am I here?" she asks. "Come on, you should know better. You've been in here plenty of times before."

"I have?"

"You have. You don't remember it, but you have."

"Before all of this?" I ask.

"Yes. This is the first time I've been here, though. I like it."

"Will you come back?" I ask.

"No," she says, and that saddens me.

"Oh."

"But tell me how you're doing."

"I've been better," I say, and she laughs.

"Preaching to the choir, man," she says. "How's

Greg holding up?"

"I haven't been able to see him. I don't know how he'll react, especially now."

"Maybe he won't remember," she says, giving a nonchalant shrug.

"Not funny," I say.

"He'll need some time. I'm kind of a big deal, after all."

"It still hasn't quite hit me yet," I say.

"Duh," she says. "Why do you think I'm here? You have the affinity for seeing dead people."

"Your funeral hasn't happened yet," I say.

"And yet, here I am. You used to see your dad too, Aaron."

"I'm Derek."

"You're Aaron," she replies. "But you want to be called Derek because you don't want to be seen as any different than you were before."

"I'm pretty sure I'm Derek," I say, getting defensive.

"But you're not. Physically yes—you occupy the same body that Derek did, but Derek died. You're Derek reborn. You're Aaron. Always will be. You've never known Derek."

The words echo in my head. *You've never known Derek.*

"So I'll never be who I want to be," I say after a minute.

"No. But I don't know why you'd want to be. Derek was a nice guy. But you're different. It took Derek twenty-five years to be a man. It took you just a few months to grow up and learn, and do what needs to be done. Look, Aaron, your life started with tragedy, but that tragedy doesn't have to define you."

"It doesn't."

"But it does. You don't talk about your leg much, and you never talk about your scars, but I know it bothers you. I know you feel like less of a person because there's something that's wrong with you. Something that will never really go away."

She pauses.

"But that's not why I'm here. I'm here because you only dream about people you've lost. Your dad, and me."

"I've only lost two people?" I ask.

"Only two that mattered. You'll get it eventually," she says, and she stands up and heads to the door. She stops and turns to face me. "Aaron, Greg loves you. He's going through a difficult process. I know this is new to you, but do what you can to help him through. It's not easy. Take it from me. I'm dead."

She hugs me, and leaves.

CHAPTER THIRTY-ONE

The hospital calls me and says that Greg is awake and can have visitors.

I walk into his room slowly, closing the door behind me, and I hold my hand up and try to smile. He's in a room by himself, the bed stationed next to the window, and I take a seat in the chair next to him. You could look at Greg and immediately think "Yeah, he's been in a car accident," with his bruised face, a cast on his left arm, and his leg raised high in traction.

"How are you holding up?" I ask.

"I'm alive, so that's not much to brag about." His voice is weak and groggy, and he's not really looking at me. "You didn't bring any food, did you?" I shake my head. "The food in here is awful; they'll force feed you that stuff if it kills you."

"Not really how it works," I mutter.

"I'm glad you're here," he says, "but where's Hayley?" He's looking right at me.

"She's not here," I say. "She, uh—no one told you?"

"Told me what?" he asks, his forehead wrinkling. "Where is she?"

"Listen," I say, leaning forward and trying not to look him in the eye, the words desperately trying to stay in my throat. "Hayley was thrown from the car that night. She must not have been wearing a seatbelt. It was too late when I got there." Greg's face scrunches up and turns red as he clenches his fist and I can tell he's getting ready to yell.

"The doctors say she didn't feel a thing!" I lie. "Shh, Greg, it's okay!" But his heart-rate is getting faster and faster and he's moaning and spittle is escaping from his mouth as he tries to thrash around in his limited position, and I slam my hand awkwardly on the call button and yell "Nurse!" unsure if I can hold him down for fear of injuring him more. *"Nurse!"*

Watching his face turn from confusion, to fear, to sadness.

"Greg I'm sorry, she's gone."

Turns to despair.

A nurse and a doctor open the door and rush forward to help, and Greg's yelling so loud that the room above must hear him, and I back away slowly, staring.

Turns to rage.

Greg pounds his fists into the bed and screams louder, the nurses come in and they try and hold him back on his bed and when he's finally quiet it's from a sedative. He lays back on the bed and gives me one final look of agony before he's asleep.

**

Hayley's body is covered in a white dress, her hands folded over her stomach. Not a trace of blood. No broken bones. At peace. This is how she looked at the funeral home. Here and now, the coffin has been closed forever. Hayley will never be seen again. Not by me, not by Greg. Not by anybody.

Few people were at the funeral. It was a short service so ten people could cry to themselves and the pallbearers who don't belong carried my friend out to the hearse and I followed behind them. Greg, stuck in the hospital, told me to take flowers. The pallbearers walk away from the grave, leaving just the priest, and myself. He says a prayer but you can see in his face that even he doesn't believe it, and he nods towards me before walking away.

I reach down and touch the dirt, hoping for some supernatural connection, but there's none.

"Hi Hayley," I say. "I'm sorry you're gone. You were the sweetest girl I ever met. You didn't seem very special at the time, but I was proven wrong, wasn't I?" I clear my throat, my eyes watering. "The more I got to know you, the more I saw just how amazing you are. Were. You helped us all grow into who we were supposed to be. You helped me. I lost everything. I died."

I pause and swallow the lump in my throat.

"You knew who I was before, and when I came back, you helped me become the new person I was designed to be. I had no chance of making it without you. When I came back, I didn't know anybody. I didn't want help from anyone. Including Greg. Including Sam. You took me under your wing and showed me who I really was, before I even knew it. You saw right through me. You resurrected me. And everyone back there at the service sat there with nothing. I feel sorry for them. They don't know anything about grief. They have no idea what it's like to know someone who is truly great. But I do."

"That was beautiful," says a voice from behind me.

I turn and see a twenty-something woman sitting on a headstone, her black hair swept to the side, and wearing a dark green dress. She walks toward me.

"Thanks," I say.

"You must be Derek," she says.

"And... I don't know you."

"I'm Lucy," she says, extending her hand to me. Hesitant, I shake.

"I'm sorry for your loss," I say.

"Oh, I never knew her," she says. "I knew Greg."

"How?"

"He was my boyfriend before you met him."

"I see."

She stands next to me and looks down at the freshly-moved dirt. "I came to see who it was that he fell in love with. You made her sound so wonderful."

"She was," I say quietly. I look back at the ground.

"I know what it's like to be misunderstood. I've been forgotten about. I've been thrown away. She really cared for you, and you really cared for her."

I try to nod but I'm frozen, tears forming in my eyes again.

"She was clearly lucky to have someone like you," she says.

"I was lucky to know her," I say.

She takes a step back. "I enjoyed hearing you speak. It was nice."

"Thanks."

"I should probably go," she says. "Maybe I'll see you around."

"Maybe," I say, and she leaves.

I go to see Greg in the hospital and I give him flowers too. He says he likes them but I doubt he likes anything right now. I tell him the funeral was nice, but I don't say anything else about Hayley. I just sit there, silent. I start reading a book I picked up earlier this morning, and as he hits the pain pump he asks me to read aloud.

Once he's asleep, I read a different book.

**

The days pass and Greg is set in his efforts to get out of the hospital since the doctors told Greg of his coming medical bills.

As I watch Greg amble around, I've found new respect for Greg. With Hayley's funeral and everything that's happened to me, he's had to deal with a lot. More than I can fathom. Greg lost the person he loved more than anyone or anything. And here I am, sitting on the bench outside his room, eating his ice cream and watching Greg start to fall but catch himself, swearing at the nurses.

He's taking everything well.

Sometimes it takes longer for Greg to get back to his feet than others, but he does it all the same, and for that, I admire him. The life Greg leads is a difficult one. Now it's my turn to take care of him.

Finally the day comes, and I open the door for him and he dumps himself in the passenger seat in my car, and pulls the door shut. He's not smiling. I walk around the other side and get in.

"Ready?" I ask, looking sideways at him as I turn

the key. He doesn't say anything. "It's all turning around now." He's still silent.

CHAPTER THIRTY-TWO

Sitting on the dirt in front of her grave again, as I've done nearly every day this week, I'm pulling up grass and throwing it aside. The flowers are now gone from her plot, taken by whoever decided they were no longer fit for presentation.

"I've decided that things aren't so bad," I say. An opening in the clouds reveals the sun in all its golden glory, shining down around me. "Once you add everything up, I mean. Sure, things are a little bad, there's no denying that. But looking at everything as a whole.."

I stand up and walk back down the path, the sun warming my back.

I get back to the apartment and Olivia is waiting for me out front, and rushes forward to stop me. "Don't go in," she says, "the police are waiting for you!"

"What? Why?" I ask.

"It's Greg!"

"He told them," I say. "I should leave, then, right?"

"I don't know!" she says, running a hand through her hair, anxious, and she freezes. I turn to follow her gaze, and see a police car pulling up at the curb, and the two officers inside are staring at *me*.

"Should I run or not?"

"Go!"

I turn and look left and right, panicking, and as the cops open their car doors I turn around and run as fast as my poor legs can carry me, the cops behind yelling for me to stop. But I don't. I keep running. I'm quickly out of breath and getting tired and I haven't even made it more than a block before the officers catch up to me and I hit the ground. They hold my arms behind me and handcuff my wrists.

Police cars are uncomfortable.

Greg comes to the window and glares at me. "You deserve all of this," he says. I guess we're not friends anymore.

Olivia lands on the seat next to me, having soared through the door.

"I'm coming with you," she says. "I don't want to have to find you again."

They take us to the police station and escort me through the large building, crowded with people for some reason, and suddenly I can't see Olivia anymore, no matter which way I look. The officer holding my arm jabs me in the ribs and says "Hurry up." They take me to an interrogation room, but it takes us a long time to walk there so I suspect they're trying to sneak me into jail.

An officer with an obscured name tag sits me down at the cold metal table and secures my handcuffs to it before leaving. The infamous two-way mirror faces me, and I've barely had the thought that I'll be waiting for a while when the door opens and in comes a man with a visitors badge carrying a folder and he sits down opposite me.

"Good to see you, Derek. You look well." He flips open the folder and looks through the loose papers.

"I'm sorry?"

"What?" he says, confused, looking up at me.

"Do I know you?" I ask.

"Derek, it's me," and he puts his hands on his chest. "Dr. Laien. You know *me*. You've been my patient for a long time."

"I've never seen you before in my life," I say.

Dr. Laien's impersonator takes a pen and scribbles some words on the paper, saying them as he writes: "Patient's memory seems to have declined over time."

"*No!*" I bark at him. "You're *not* Dr. Laien."

"Derek when was the last time you took your medicine?" he asks calmly.

"You didn't give me any!"

He scribbles again. "Patient refuses to take prescribed medication."

"*What?!*" I'm furious now.

"Derek, you need to calm down," he says, unperturbed by my reactions.

"Tell me who you are!"

"This is no way to behave Derek, you're in enough trouble as it is, and we haven't even discussed why you're here."

"Please, enlighten me," I say, disgusted.

"Mr. Kailer called me a few days ago and informed me of your excursions with the recently deceased Mrs. Kailer, and his concerns about it, and I too share those concerns."

"Is that so?" I say through gritted teeth.

"I'd like to ask you some questions," he says.

"I want a lawyer," I say.

"I'm afraid that's not possible," he says, his eyes unblinking.

We just stare at each other, before he seems to remember what he's doing and looks back at his folder. "I'd like to ask you these questions, if that's alright with you."

"I'm handcuffed to a table," I say. "I'm all yours."

"Good choice," he says, a smile creeping along his face. "Now! These are basic questions, and all I expect are 'yes' or 'no' answers. Understood?"

I nod.

"I need you to answer 'yes' or 'no', Derek."

"Fine," I say. "Yes."

"Excellent. First question: you've been seeing realistic apparitions of deceased people, am I to understand that?"

I don't say anything.

"Derek, you need to answer these. It's more important than you realize."

I take my time before sighing, and saying "Yes."

"Good. And is it true that you can successfully communicate with them?"

"Yes."

"Okay, now I'd like some minor explanations. How long have you been able to communicate with these visions?"

"A long time," I say.

"I need an exact date."

"I don't know."

"Longer than a year?" he asks.

"Just a few months." He's writing down everything I say.

"Were you able to communicate with them as soon as you saw them?"

"Yes."

"And what did you tell them?"

"To get out of my house," I say. I'm staring him dead in the eye.

"Interesting. And what did they say to you?"

"They told me that they were dead."

"Which led to what?" he asks. I'm wondering how many people are standing behind the glass, and when I look away I notice the camera in the corner, but the recording light is off.

"They told me where they were buried."

"And?" He knows. He just needs me to say it for whatever record. I have an idea of what this is for, but I don't want to think about it.

"I reburied them."

"I see," he says, and he stands up, facing the mirror. "Do you know why I'm asking you these questions?"

"Please, tell me," I say.

"When Mr. Kailer told me what you've been up to, I must admit it was surprising. So I had some of my police friends do some investigating. Mr. Kailer had names of the apparitions you claim to have encountered, so they checked on their burial sites. The graves themselves had been tampered with, and in the case of one mausoleum, was partially destroyed, somehow. Mr. Kailer and myself took that information to a judge, and he requested some clarification, which you have just given me."

I don't say anything.

"So, with what I've just told you, do you care to

guess what this is about?"

"Why don't you just tell me? You seem excited about it, so go ahead."

"With the information you just provided, I can persuade Judge Franks to have you committed to Hawkins Memorial."

"Hawkins Memorial?" I ask, but he doesn't seem to hear me.

"Of course, there's the preliminary seventy-two hour evaluation to determine if you truly belong in a mental health institution, like Mr. Kailer and I think you do." A sly smile appears on his face. "but it won't take much to convince them."

My jaw is clenched and I'm starting to shake from anger.

"Why isn't the camera recording?" I ask, nodding my head in its direction.

His smirk falters and he anxiously glances towards the camera.

"Is Greg paying you?"

"Someone has to pay me," he says.

"Is Greg paying the cops involved?" I'm past furious, now.

"Nothing wrong with the officers making some extra income."

"Unless they're claiming I'm insane and deserve to be locked up!" I yell at him, livid.

"You *are* insane!" he yells back, slamming his palms on the table.

"Tell me your real name," I say quietly.

He stands up, wearing a sympathetic smile and backing away, retreating to the door. "I have some phone calls to make. You're in for rough night, Mr. Wilson. Try and make the best of it." He leaves.

I'm left by myself for a long time before someone comes in and disconnects me from the table. He leads me through the building to a cell where there's a pile of clothes waiting for me; thin bluish-gray shirt and pants combination.

"Put those on," the officer says.

After I do, he handcuffs me and takes me by the arm to the rear of the station where an unmarked white van is waiting. The panel slides open and the officer jerks his head towards it. "Get in."

The van takes me to Hawkins Memorial where my arms are held by two orderlies at all times as my information is being taken down by a female doctor. Dr. Williams, the badge reads. I figure it's best if I don't say anything yet and just ride it out until I'm officially supposed to talk. A guy who rode in the van with me is talking to her in hushed voices, and she waves her hand at the orderlies beside me and they guide me down hall after hall until there's an open door and they push me inside, slamming the door behind me.

"We'll come for you in the morning," a gruff voice says, and then all I hear is footsteps.

The room is exactly how I pictured. The thick, ribbed, padded white walls, the bland ceiling, the small cot in the corner that I know will be more uncomfortable than anything I've ever touched.

I lay down on the cot, grimacing, and as I stare up at the blank ceiling I let out a long breath, stunted by adrenaline.

"I guess it's not so bad."

CHAPTER THIRTY-THREE

Water splashes on my face and someone yells "Wake up, Sixth Sense!" Half-asleep and shivering, I try to blink my eyes into focus. He's a big guy, or at least he looks like he is, and he lifts me to my feet by my shirt. "We've got things to do, today."

He and another guy walk me down to a large door with a plaque that says "Dr. Williams" on it. The guy on my right reaches out and knocks. There's a loud buzz, and he pushes the door open. The two release me and back out of the office, closing the door behind them. The room is wall to wall bookshelves, with a desk close to one wall and a chair that holds Dr. Williams, and an empty chair on the other side.

Dr. Williams herself is sitting forward, leaning on the desk, and smiling. There's a manila folder in front of her which I'm guessing is my file.

"Please, sit down," she says, gesturing to the chair in front of me. I sit.

"Hello Derek, I'm Dr. Williams. I'm in charge of this facility, and you'll be staying with us for a few days."

"Sounds like a dream vacation," I say, dryly.

"I can understand why you're unhappy about this —"

"I don't think you do," I say. "I'm not supposed to be here."

"No one is ever supposed to be here," she says.

"Greg set me up!" I say. "He hired people to forge

documents about me and have me locked up here!"

"Forge documents? Even these?" and she pulls out large photos from the folder and places them before me. They're of graves, freshly dug, and a mausoleum. My projects.

I don't say anything.

"Derek, you're here because your friend is worried about you, and with your spoken testimony on what you've been doing... I want to make sure you're healthy enough to be on your own." She leans forward again. "Is there anything you think I should know before we get started here?"

I shake my head. "No."

"Good. I have a colleague coming in a few hours and he'll be assisting in this process, and helping us run some tests."

"What kind of tests?" I ask.

"Just some standard stuff to make sure there's nothing out of the ordinary," she says.

"Like—"

"Until then, you're free to spend time in our community room and interact with the other patients." She smiles a sickly sweet smile and presses a button to her right. The door opens and in walk the two orderlies, large and impressive, ready to work. Lurch and Gronk.

"Do you guys come in a group rate?" I ask them as the door closes. Lurch punches me in my gut and they half-heartedly lift me off the floor and drag me down the hall.

I'm deposited in a large room, like a sterile common room, already occupied by maybe twenty other people who, from the looks of it, have been here for years, some probably decades. There's a few tables hugging the walls, and a couch positioned in front of a TV playing one of those shopping channels. I scan the room, trying to decide who I should sit next to, and I settle on just going to sit at a table by myself, holding my stomach, which feels like it might fall apart.

I look at these miserable souls around me; no light behind their eyes, blank stares, sagging jaws, almost everyone sporting unkempt, dirty rats nests for hair, and just sitting around, like they're dead.

My eyes never leave the TV, and I must have watched several hours of it, but I can feel the gaze of at least one orderly standing by the door. A female orderly enters the room and announces it's time for medication. I watch the drones form a sloppy line in the middle of the room, and I have a sudden urge to join them. I stand up and walk towards them, but my legs slow down and I'm falling forward.

I wake up and watch ceiling tiles scroll past me, like falling blocks. My stomach is knotted and I feel terrible.

Gronk is walking beside me. I must be on a gurney. He looks down at me.

"Good, you're awake," he says. "We were worried about you."

"What happened?" I ask, my voice barely there.

"You passed out. We moved up some of the other tests to make sure you're okay."

I turn my head and I can read some of the signs next to the doors we pass. Examination Room A, with B right next door. Gronk leads me to the very end of the hall, dead ended with double doors with no label.   Not eerie at all.

He pushes the gurney through them to reveal a narrow room with a window spanning the length of the room showing a second room containing an MRI machine, and a door at the end. Standing on my other side by the wall is Dr. Williams and a man I don't recognize.

"Oh good, I was hoping you'd be awake when you got here," says Dr. Williams. "Derek, this is Dr. Raden." She gestures to the other guy, who nods. "How are you feeling?" she asks.

"Not bad," I groan.

"Well we'll soon know for sure," says Dr. Williams. "We're going to give you an MRI for our first test. This isn't how we usually do things, but under the current circumstances, we felt it was necessary to alter our priorities. All you need to do is change into a gown and you'll be ready, okay?"

I nod.

Gronk hands me a gown and they let me into the other room where I change. I climb onto the sliding table, and Dr. Raden tells me to lie still, and that I should try to get comfortable. He hands me ear plugs, and he places what he calls an antenna over my head.

The machine buzzes on and the table slides in.

A half hour later I'm sitting on a bench outside the room with Lurch standing by the door. I guess Gronk had more pressing business. The door opens and Dr. Williams pops her head out.

"Derek, we'll have to continue this later. Larry, could you take Derek back to his room?"

Lurch nods.

"And give him something to do. Pencil and paper should be fine."

"Is something wrong?" I ask.

"We'll resume our tests tomorrow, Derek. Get some rest." The door closes.

Lurch maintains a loose grip on my arm as we walk, as if he's lost interest. Once back in my room, he closes the door eliminating most of the light. There's a notepad with a pencil on the floor by my feet. I pick them up and sit down on my bed, and start to write in the poor light. Paragraphs and paragraphs, killing time with words that mean nothing more than the passing of time.

I hear footsteps get louder and louder and voices trying to be quiet. Someone knocks on the door and it swings open, the noon light flooding in.

Dr. Williams walks in, followed by Greg, and the door closes again, but not before someone ducks in before it's dark again. It's Olivia! She's found me! Dr. Williams is holding a folder and steps forward, sitting down on the ground in front of me. Greg stays standing by the door, and Olivia sits on the bed next to me, and puts her arm on my shoulder. Neither of us say anything. She almost looks worried.

"Why are you here?" I ask Greg.

"I asked him to be here," says Dr. Williams.

"Why?"

"Derek, we've found something." She takes a deep breath. "Your MRI showed some irregularities in your brain tissue." She pauses, opens her mouth, looking away, and back at me. "Derek, your brain is dying."

"Excuse me?" I say. She hands me the folder and I open it, revealing a handful of x-rays. "This is my brain?"

Dr. Williams nods. "It's called Parasin Dysplasia. It means your brain is dying, a bit at a time. According to the MRI, you've lost one section already, and part of another. It's why you fainted today. Your brain was working harder than normal, which can cause your brain to wither away faster than usual."

I stare at the sheet.

Parasin Dysplasia. My brain is rotting away. The tissue is fading to black, restricting my memories, my thoughts, my movements. My mind is trying to kill me.

"It can take weeks, months, years, to kick in, and even after that, once it does start working, it can take any matter of time. In your case, it looks like it's been attacking for weeks, at an alarming rate."

"What can we do about it?" I ask her.

"Unfortunately there is no treatment."

"None?"

"That's correct," she says. "I'm also sorry to tell you that I don't think you have much time at all."

Silence fills the room.

"I'll leave the rest to you, Mr. Kailer." says Dr. Williams, standing back up. Greg moves aside and Dr. Williams knocks on the door. It opens, and she leaves.

I can only imagine the conversation they all had without me. Even Olivia was probably there.

"There's no treatment," I say. "Sounds amazing."

"I'm sorry, Derek," says Olivia, patting my arm.

"But now you're here," I say, looking at Greg. "What could you possibly have to say to me?"

"You know," he says. "I spent a lot of money to put you in here." He walks to the wall and leans his back against it, sliding down until he's sitting. He looks up and down the walls, taking it in.

"Dr. Williams was on board once we had a court order prefaced by a sworn statement from my hired Dr. Laien on your verbal testimony. She's so willing to help. It was almost too easy to enjoy."

He clears his throat. "But then this thought started to eat at me. This fear— this idea that maybe you were right. Maybe you're not crazy. Maybe Hayley trusted you for a reason. You were so confident, after all, with no other signs of being insane. Even as big as the one sign was. I decided that I needed to know: Did she believe a lie? Or did she follow the truth?" He shifts his legs and moves forward so he's less than two feet from me. "And you want to know what caused me to second guess myself?"

I don't say anything.

"Something hit me. Like, a person. As if someone ran into me, in my own house," and you can hear the fear in his voice.

"I punched him," says Olivia. I smile.

"Tell me, Derek. She died because of my anger at you. Tell me she didn't die for a lie. Were they *real*?"

I nod my head.

"And you could talk to them, and they could talk to you?" he breathes.

"Yes," I say. "But you don't need my answers, do you? You met one."

I can see the whites of his eyes now. "When I was hit!"

"Greg, meet Olivia." And she punches him again, knocking him on his butt.

His eyes are so wide now that I know he's nothing short of terrified. "It's all true..." He nods his head feverishly, and scrambles to his feet. He grabs my arm and pulls me up. He walks over to the door and knocks on it. "Come on, I'm getting you out of here."

"*What?*" I don't move.

"He's serious," says Olivia. "He has a plan."

- 239 -

"I got you in here, I can get you out," he says, and the door opens. Lurch, caught off guard, is punched in the face by Greg, and topples over. Dr. Williams is standing by, too shocked to move. Greg grabs her by and shoves her into the room before closing the door on her. *"Come on!"* he hisses, and I follow him out the door.

"Do you have a plan?" I ask him as we rush down the hall.

"Kind of," he says back. I throw a look at Olivia, who shrugs.

He motions for me to slow down as we come to an intersecting hallway, and we move on. Hallway after hallway, and I'm sure Greg has no idea where he's going, but then we come to a sign that points to the main entrance, and I feel some glimmer of hope, until we come to the turn and Dr. Raden is standing right in front of us.

"Derek?" he says, confused. "Mr.—" and Greg shoves him so hard that he trips over his coat and falls flat on his back with a loud thud.

"I think someone probably heard that," says Olivia.

"Let's go!" says Greg, and he rushes around the corner into the main hall, where the receptionist is standing by the desk, concerned about Dr. Raden's current situation.

"Excuse me," she says. "Where are you taking that patient?" Greg freezes. I look at Olivia, to say that she should do something, but the receptionist takes the moment to quickly pick up the phone and call over the loudspeaker "CODE FOUR: MAIN ENTRANCE." and it's too late by the time Olivia runs forward and pushes her right over the desk. Olivia turns to look at us, grimacing, and says "I think she'll be okay, eventually."

Greg looks as though he's caught somewhere between impressed and being petrified, so I grab his arm and push him forward. We make it out of the building and

Greg points to the side towards a car—hey, *my* car!

"You brought my car?" I ask.

"Seemed like a cool idea: breaking you out in your own car," he says, unlocking the door.

We get in, and he peels out, screaming towards the main gate which is closing, fast, but he rams right into it, throwing us forward but still making it through, leaving parts of my car along the driveway.

"Sorry," says Greg. "Thought your car was sturdier than that."

"At least it worked," I say. "So what's the plan now?"

"Well," he says. "Places like Hawkins don't take kindly to people leaving before they're due, especially when it's a court order, and it'll be a long time before anyone decides to look and see if it's fake. We should switch cars, and drive a long way away."

"Where to?" I ask, glancing back at Olivia in the backseat.

"Where do you want to go?"

"I haven't seen the East Coast yet."

"Sounds perfect," he says.

We turn down a side street just as police cars race by the other way, sirens blasting.

"Greg?" I say.

"Yeah?" he replies.

"I forgive you." I mean it.

He smiles. "It might be a little too late on my part, but I forgive you too."

We ditch my car and take Greg's neighbor's car, to

which apparently he has access for whatever reason he might need. ("Timmy just doesn't care who uses it, he's kind of stupid that way.")

We drive for hours and hours on end. Greg pumps gas, and Olivia stays with me in the car.

"This wasn't how I pictured helping people," I say.

"Being arrested doesn't really fit into anyone's life goals," she says.

"But we helped some, though."

"You did a good job," she says.

"Did you ever find any more?" I ask.

"Not even one."

"I guess we won't, now."

"You've done your part," she says.

"I guess so. I'm sorry I can't help you."

"It's my own fault," she says. "I should have had her do it, whether I wanted to go or not."

The driver's door opens and Greg gets in. "Okay," he says. "Thirteen hours to go, and we're there."

I try to sleep most of the way, but I steadily feel worse and worse. Headaches come and go, and each one that comes is more painful than the last, and Ibuprofen does nothing to help.

When I do fall asleep, it's not for long, and I wake up with a twisted feeling in my stomach like I'm going to be sick. It's around eight in the morning when I tell Greg that he needs to pull over and let me out. I stumble to a small patch of grass on the side of the road and I fall down.

"Derek!" I hear someone call. The grass is a vibrant shade of green, and slightly blurry. Muffled footsteps grow louder and I can feel the impact on the ground, and I feel hands touching me, rolling me over to look up at the sky. Greg's face is right in front of my own, his hand under my head, holding me up. "Derek, are you okay?"

"Never better," I say, and my gut makes an awful noise.

"Come on, Derek, you're okay. You're okay."

And there's Olivia standing over me.

"I don't think you have to run from the police anymore," I mumble.

"I wasn't running from them," he says. "I was getting you to the coast so you could have a nice last few days."

"You knew, didn't you?"

"Williams called me and told me over the phone," he says. "She just wanted me there to help tell you. I just had something different in mind."

Olivia gets on her knees and leans over me.

"Thank you," she says. "You made this more bearable than I ever could have imagined. I'm glad to have known you."

"Olivia," I say. Even I can tell I won't be here much longer. "You were the best of me. Thank you."

Another car has pulled up behind Greg's oddly parked car and curious passerby are coming up to see what's going on.

But Greg's and Olivia's faces are starting to fade as my breathing slows down. The ground doesn't feel so cool anymore, the sun warming me, the blue sky overreaching and extending down to me. My head turns sideways to look at the grass but the grass isn't there, so I look back up and the blue is succumbing to the light of the sun, burning bright and over saturated with fire, and everything around me erupts into flames, engulfing me.

And I'm in a metal chair. I'm sitting in a metal chair at a metal table, outside a café. This place looks strangely familiar. I see my reflection in the café windows. My face isn't scarred. I raise my hand to touch my face and my hand is complete. I pull up my pants leg and my leg is whole. I lean back in my chair, and let out a long breath.

"This is insane," I say.

"It's pretty weird up here, but it just got a lot better," a voice says. Hayley and my dad are standing next to me, and they sit down at my table, smiling.

"Hi Aaron," says Hayley.

"It's good to see you again," my dad says.

The End.

To the people who provided important critique, advice and encouragement, this work would have never made it past the first few paragraphs. Thank you.

Special thanks to my Alpha and Beta Readers:
Addy Play
Anna Flynn
Brian Oswinkle
Brittany Kramer
David Kuriny
Diana Leininger
Elizabeth Leininger
Jessica Smith
Joanna Mauler
Julia Lyall
Kaleigh Wernick
Kayla Ward
Liam Renner
Ryan Leubecker
Sarah Zeller
Tunde Ogunfolaju

I would like to extend my utmost thanks to my editors, Dad and Mom, because this book wouldn't have gotten anywhere without you.

Indiegogo Supporters
Aaron Miller
Barry Gilman
Beth Casagrande
Brian Oswinkle
Courtney Sobus
Crystal Wagner
Daniel C Loizeaux
Devon Richards

Emily Leonard
Evan Fuller
Greg and Erin Beerli
Hannah Carr
Hannah M Johnson
Jay Reid
Jeff Soule
Jeffrey A Brown
Jeremiah H Medley
Jordan Fuller
Julia R Lyall
Karlie Bartholomew
Katrina Dunne
Kelley Seisman
Lindey Allen
Lois Gray
Marc Martinex
Marcus Hague
Rebecca Lamoreux
Sarah Zeller
Tina Lamoreux
Timothy Shaffer
Tim Torre